The Least Weasel

What You Believe ...

Joseph McConnell

ProcArch LLC, Ann Arbor

ISBN: 978-0-9886913-5-3

First edition, 2014.

The headings are scientific and common names for mammals that are not, as of the time of writing, yet extinct. Let's try to keep it that way. According to Genesis, Penuel is the name Jacob gave to the place where he wrestled with an Angel.

This is a work of fiction. All characters in this work are inventions and they do not represent real people. The Ann Arbor Police Department, the Grosse Pointe Park Department of Public Safety, the FBI, and the University of Michigan Police Department do not have personnel such as those described here nor are the procedural details necessarily accurate. The AAPD and the UMDP, to the author's knowledge, do not dislike each other. And if they did, how would the author know?

This book is for Linda and for the memory of Raegan who would, I hope, have enjoyed it.

Preface: Stories and Beliefs

Stories are important to human beings. Besides being entertaining, they sometimes teach things, sometimes they lay down the law, occasionally they're comforting, and most of all, they lay out a set of beliefs common to some group or other. Whether or not the group in question is yours or somebody else's seems not to matter; I don't have a lot in common with ninth-century Danes, but I find a lot in *Beowulf* to agree with.

Because of the way we think evolution works, we think that humans developed and refined a literary ability in response to some kind of need. If we agree on that, and if we believe that all species evolve under the same general set of rules, it follows that other species besides ourselves might have evolved story-telling, too. It would have to have been of some advantage to them, and they would have needed a couple of prerequisites: self-awareness and a means of communication. Experiments are beginning to tell us that dogs are at least somewhat self-aware, and from body language to vocalizations, they do communicate. Based on long personal experience with dogs, it wouldn't surprise me at all if they have a body of literature, oral, I grant you, since they don't seem to have a written language, but still there.

I wanted to test this idea, and since I've heard repeatedly that dogs have about the same intellectual power as human two to four year olds (depending on which study you read and on which day of the week it is), I started with a control group, interviewing a human, age four.

McConnell: Do you like stories?

Four-year-old: Yes.

M: You like hearing stories?

FYO: Yes. I like bedtime stories.

M: Do you ever tell stories?

FYO: Sometimes I tell ... I tell about the dogs.

M: The dogs?

FYO: Yes. There was a girl and the dogs.

M: Did she live with the dogs?

FYO: Yes, and she lived with them in ... in ... a dog house!

M: Wasn't she cold?

FYO: No. And she lived in the dog house with ... three dogs.

M: Why did she have to live in the dog house?

FYO: Because ... she had ... she had ... she had to tell them stories.

M: Got it. Did anything bad ever happen?

FYO: No. I don't like bad stories.

With that data set as a baseline, I then shifted to the primary group and conducted what was intended to be a parallel interview with a dog.

McConnell: Do you like stories?

Dog: Human stories or dog stories?

M: Well ... how about a human story with dogs in it?

D: Do you know what time it is?

M: Yes, it's ... ten after three.

D: Not dinnertime yet, then?

M: No, not quite.

D: Okay. Just asking.

M: You said "dog stories". Do dogs tell stories?

D: We sometimes tell each other what to watch out for. Bigger dogs, bears. Cars.

M: How do you do that?

D: Okay, let's say there's a bear over there (points with nose). And a puppy didn't see it. I'd growl and make my hair stand up ... like this. Do you know what's for dinner, by the way?

M: Ah, I think it's dog food.

D: Great!

M: So dogs believe bears are dangerous?

D: Sure. Don't you?

M: Well, I don't meet many bears, frankly.

D: I don't either, but still ...

Beliefs. The human child believes that in a universe he controls, bad things don't happen, and if he's telling the story, it's his universe. The dog believes that larger carnivores present a danger; he's never seen a bear, but he's prepared, and he prepares a puppy, too. The story I have to tell here in this book is probably for neither the child nor the dog. It's a bad story, much of it, in the child's sense, and a bit more complicated than the dog cares about. It's about beliefs, some common,

3

some unique, and some dangerous. We aren't taught, when we're puppies, to growl and raise our hackles when we see a dangerous belief; we should be.

Vulpus velox The Swift Fox

The wind drove a snow shower against the west faces of the office buildings: fine-grained flakes and sleet. Inside any structure with more than three stories, people could feel a slight quiver each time the wind gusted. Low clouds moved with the wind, making Ann Arbor in January a dark and depressing place.

In her office, Colleen MacArthur rattled out the last email message of the morning and glanced at the time. A quarter after twelve: time for lunch and checking personal messages. Her smart phone showed only one, a note from her husband's old colleague, Jenn Langton. The title was just "What do you think?" They'd been talking frequently in the last month; Colleen was the most effective business woman Jenn knew, and her advice was valuable.

The message said "Got a call last night. They caved in. Offer was everything we talked about, plus a bit. Slightly better salary than I asked for and a lot better bonus. Everything else was what I asked for. Plus, got another offer. From the FBI. Got a minute to talk?"

Although she was hungry, Colleen couldn't resist calling. She knew what Jenn wanted to talk about, and her own curiosity was intense. Jenn was a good friend of hers and an even better friend of her husband, Mac. She called.

"Are you in the middle of something?"

"No," said Jenn, "This is a good time, actually."

"So the recruiter got Holcombe to just roll over and sign up?"

"That's what it looks like. I suppose that means I didn't ask for enough."

"Well, still ... that's great. They really want you. But tell me about the FBI."

"They're, um, proposing a merger. With collocation. Here. At the Ann Arbor office, I guess, initially. And then we'd find a new site as soon as we could."

"I'll be damned," said Colleen. "Were you expecting that?"

"I ... guess so. I mean, I hadn't exactly applied or anything."

"So what do you think?"

"What do *you* think?"

"I'd say, accept 'em both."

When they hung up, Jenn sat for a minute, ignoring the salad on her plate. She'd been out on the west side of town, working on a break-in case; she was now having lunch, in theory, at an old Greek diner and doughnut shop on Stadium. She wasn't really having lunch because her stomach wasn't in the greatest shape. In the next five minutes, she'd make two more phone calls and in the process, pick her life up by the heels and shake it. She sighed and tapped the contacts entry for a personnel recruiter.

He typically spent ten to twelve hours a day on the phone, and most of the time Jenn's calls went to his voicemail. This time, he was expecting (hoping, actually) for her to be in touch, and he picked up instantly. Jenn was surprised at how easy it was just to say "yes". He was extremely pleased, since he'd been trying to find someone like Jenn for the last three months, and now he'd be collecting a check from his client: five percent of a reasonable, Director-level salary. It was hard enough tracking down a candidate with law enforcement experience and whose background had no obvious security clearance problems. Finding one locally, without the issues of moving expenses, children in school, aging parents, spouses to pry loose from their own jobs: hardly to be expected. And if you did luck into someone like that, what were the odds that she'd be ready to make a change? It was damn near a miracle.

"Well," Jenn thought, "One down." She took a deep breath and tapped another phone number. This time, it rang five times and flipped over to voice mail.

"This is Andy Patel. I'm either on the phone, or I'm driving, or I just can't answer right now. Please leave me a message, and I'll get back to you."

"Hello, Agent Patel," said Jenn. "Thanks for giving me a day to think things over. The answer you're looking for is Yes! Call me, and we'll ... talk about everything. But again, yes, that's, um, I mean, the answer is *yes*."

Neofelis unca The Snow Leopard

The precise year in the Julian calendar wasn't all that important. Gaston cared far more about the months and the seasons. Years came and went without many implications, but the seasons mapped to the weather, and the weather was of prime concern. Someone with a more formal education could have told him that it was now a year in the last quarter of the seventeenth century, 1681 in fact. That person might have been a Jesuit missionary or an official of some kind; Gaston would have listened politely, drawing on a tradition of hierarchy and respect, but the information wouldn't have been especially useful. What he'd really want to know was whether he had time to make his trip before the storm season started.

Gaston was thirty, give or take a few years. He was born in a farmhouse a little to the southwest of Bayeux, in Normandy. He had memories of a place that must have been France, since there were open fields, enclosed with hedgerows. There was no terrain like that in New France. Outside the settlements, there was only forest and, until you stood on the shore of a lake, no horizon. There were Frenchmen here, certainly, and Indians, too, mostly the people lumped together as "Hurons".

Gaston came here when he was very young, coming with his mother and the soldier she followed. This man may or may not have been Gaston's father, but he accepted the role when the woman died on the voyage. Gaston asked the man when Mama would come back, and the man had said "We'll meet her in Heaven." After the ship reached port, Gaston asked "Is this Heaven?" The soldier looked at the docks, the towering rock above, the muddy streets, the snow, and the sky that was clouding up and blocking out the sun. He only sighed, and Gaston didn't ask again.

Gaston grew up around the barracks at Quebec. In his teens he went against the Iroquois on the expedition of the Marquis de Tracy. He wore the brown coat of the Regiment *Carignan-Salières* for a while, but in a lull between small, pointless wars, he drifted off into the fur trade. He became adept at handling a canoe and an axe and the other tools of the woods. The traders at Montreal knew him as quiet and responsible. Most valuable of all, he could speak with the Ojibwe and make himself understood by some of the other peoples, too. He was a man who could go into the upper lakes, keep a crew of voyageurs and Indians in line, and avoid upsetting the Jesuit priests. Or just avoid them, period. He'd been on two trips already this year, and the beaver pelts he brought back were long gone on their way to Europe.

Now he was alone with his canoe and a gun, an axe and a fur coat, boots, leggings, and a knit cap. He had food for himself and a small bag of trade goods as presents. He carried a message, committed to memory and also to paper. Gaston couldn't read, but the man he was going to see would read it, and if the paper was lost on the way, Gaston would still be able to tell him what he needed to know. It involved furs, deals, cutting another man out of a deal, and pushing far out into the west, going farther than before, farther into the stunning reaches of the lakes and the prairies beyond them. The message was a brief, primitive kind of business plan, and it was important for the field agent to receive it yet this year, so that he could start on it early in the Spring. It was late, as business plans often are, and Gaston was the only one who would agree to take it. He planned on marrying soon, and the money would go a long way toward that goal. He would go quickly, by himself, and come back with an acknowledgement. If he was lucky, if the storms held off.

The trip was familiar. It cut across the wilderness using the river *Kichi Sibi*, bringing him through a series of channels and portages, down to the shore of the *Lac des Hurons*. It cut out hundreds of leagues of coasting along the lower lakes, and it avoided weather risks to some extent. No Iroquois were likely to be raiding inland at this time of year, north of the lakes, and the poor battered Huron peoples were friends.

He followed the river, paddling north against the stream, trying to make good time. Earlier in the year, there would have been traffic, Voyageurs and company crews, Ojibwe, Menominee from the other side of the straits, heading up or down, going up with trade goods or down with furs. Now, the river was empty, and only a few of the riverside camps were occupied.

Only after Meeting-of-the-Waters, where the trade left the *Kichi Sibi* and went west on the *Mattawa*, through a series of streams and lakes and portages to Lake Nipissing, only then did he meet another party. Like Gaston, the man was alone, an Ojibwe from the north shore of the greatest of the lakes, taking one last bundle of beaver pelts down to Montreal. He was elderly, tired, and cold, discouraged that he'd be spending the winter in the town. He and Gaston had spoken last year, and they camped together now, making a fire that would keep wolves away through the night, and telling the news of the last season. In the morning, Gaston made the older man a gift of a trade knife, replacing one that he'd fumbled and dropped in deep water. In return, the Indian promised to tell the trader at Montreal that he'd met Gaston and that all was well.

The weather stayed clear as Gaston went on, getting colder but only once or twice dusting the trees with snow. His pace slowed because this river had more rapids and falls to portage around. By himself, it took two trips each time, once carrying the canoe and once with his gear. "*If I had a wife ...*" he thought. With the money from this trip, perhaps he would. He had a girl in mind, three-quarters French, one-quarter Ojibwe, and she'd already had her brush with the smallpox. She was healthy and woods-smart, and she smiled nicely. It would be good to have someone to talk to.

When the Mattawa River left him, finally, at Nipissing, he crossed the lake in a day, took the mouth of the French River, and felt the usual relief of being halfway done. He ran down it quickly. There were fewer portages; here and there, it twisted and turned and became a braided stream, but at the last, it ran almost straight past *Isle des Cochons* and out through a maze of rocks and small islands into the huge lobe of Lake Huron, the water that would later be called Georgian Bay. He'd been fifteen days getting there.

The sun was going down, making each small wave a black triangle on a silver surface. Gaston had seen calm weather on the big lakes, and it always gave a quick feeling of confidence. The waters were welcoming, and it seemed a bit less cold, too, with no breeze blowing. He made his simple camp, built the inevitable fire in a circle of charcoal left over from someone else's, and he ate. He fed the fire again, rolled himself in a pair of blankets, and slept in the lee of his canoe. He woke only once in the night, when the wind increased. He put more wood on the camp fire and went back to sleep.

In the morning, his confidence vanished. The western sky was gray, and there was a dark bar across the horizon. It could be just cold and rain, or it could be the first storm. He stood for minutes, staring at the gathering weather and calculating the distance he could go before it arrived. He looked at the water, judging the waves, remembering other trips along this shore. If the wind blew up, it would at least blow from the west, pushing him toward the shore and not out onto the open lake. But the shore was dangerous. It was a tangle of small islands and large rocks, all the way to the first real shelter behind Manitoulin, the spirit island of the Ojibwe.   Four leagues of hard paddling, maybe five, he thought. Five leagues of open water, across the wind, or perhaps twice that if he kept close to shore, dodging the rocks. His boat was the smallest type, a *canot léger*, and he could make it move quickly, but even so, the open water route would take at least five hours.

"*Noon,* " he thought. "*By noon, I will be running by the long point. Then, by that big island with no beach to land on. And after that, I'll be sheltered in the channel by the island where we caught rabbits to eat. The one with beaches all around to land on.*" He began to load his gear into the canoe.

In twenty minutes, Gaston was ready. Everything loose was lashed tightly with marline or with laces of deer hide. He launched the boat straight out from the shore and pushed it forward into the waves as he rolled in. He began paddling instantly, keeping the bow into the wind. He got quickly off shore and away from the surf zone – or the zone where there would be surf in a few hours. His stroke was strong and accustomed. If you counted them up, the miles he'd travelled in his life were mostly on water, and his ability in a canoe was instinctive. He turned and moved along the shore of his camp island, then out between two bare rocks. He cleared them, and he could see open water ahead. It was at that point that he saw a body rolling in the waves.

It was unmistakable. Each wave ducked it under, but it came back up, riding low in the water and with the arms flopping lifelessly. Gaston could see that it was wearing heavy clothes, soaked and pulling it down. It was very close. "In a minute or two," he thought, "I'll be able to see the face."

He was used to making quick decisions. In his life, they'd been fairly simple ones. Join the army or starve. Fight or flee. Argue or obey. Here, it was more complicated. There was no question of saving a life or not – the body was obviously just that: a dead body. But he must decide in the next few seconds about investigating it, trying to get it into the canoe or leaving it. Even (and this made up his mind for him) seeing if it had a face he knew. There weren't many people at all in New France, and most of his acquaintances travelled on the lakes and rivers. This body might easily be a friend or a partner or a rival. Or an enemy. What if it was an Iroquois raider? That would tell him any number of useful things.

He changed course slightly and paddled toward it, keeping the waves closely on the west side of the bow. He would get one chance to go by the body and decide what to do next. Then if he had to, he could try to come back around. "*Dangerous*," he thought. "*There could be another body in the water if I go over.*" He slowed as he got nearer. It was floating on its back now, its legs toward him. If he trailed a loop as he went by, he might be able to snag it around an ankle and then tow it – where? Not back to the camp; he rejected any loss of forward progress as adding more danger. But ahead, just a quarter league or less, was a tiny rock with a pair of cedar trees. Not an island at all, but land at least. "*Catch it with a rope as I pass, tow it behind that rock, and there'll be just enough shelter. I can at least look at him.*" (He assumed it would be a man.) "*Maybe I can even get him ashore.*"

It took twenty minutes, but Gaston managed it. Behind the islet there was a channel. It was bounded on the east by either a larger island or the mainland. It made no difference, because all he intended to do was run up on a slab of smooth rock, reel in the body, and gather all the useful information it had to offer. If it was an Iroquois, he thought, and recently dead, that would mean a late-year raid. If there were wounds, whether it was Iroquois or Ojibwe or a white man, it would mean the same bad thing: fighting had been going on somewhere nearby, and he'd have to be even more cautious about strangers than he would have been anyway. So he pulled it in closely, jumped carefully onto the wet rock shore, and dragged the canoe as far from the water as he could. Then he reeled in the body.

It was no Iroquois warrior, and it wasn't a man. The dead had been a woman, an adult woman, native, wearing a a woman's trade shirt but leggings as a man would have. She had a length of line around her waist, cinching in a wool blanket, and there was an iron knife held in place with a strip of deer skin. Her hair was worn like a man's, and only her shirt and the breasts under it showed her gender. Gaston had seen drowned men and women before, and it was clear that she'd died in the water. The blanket had probably hindered her. She looked as though she'd been strong and healthy, but if she'd been in a canoe that rolled over, if she couldn't get back to it and right it and get back in while the waves fought against her – well, that was a common and simple death. But what now?

Gaston was neither an ethnologist nor a comparative theologian. He knew the Ojibwe people had a religion of their own, but its rituals at death were a closed book to him. And many of them had converted to the Church, anyway. He could say nothing for this woman that would help or hinder her now. If she was a Christian, he should do something, but his last confession had been months back; it would be presumptuous at least, perhaps sinful. More than that, he knew nothing of the liturgy. He'd never been to a funeral where he could hear what the priest was saying, and it would have been in Latin, anyway. On the other hand, if the body had still been a follower of its own rite, she was damned already, dying without the Church's sanction. He passed over the idea that she might have been of the new religion. He'd never met a protestant but once when he and his Corporal had tended a wounded Dutchman, dying with a hatchet gash in his head and gasping nonsense in bad French about a prayer book.

There was no soil here to bury her. Just enough dirt and sand and rotted bark had gathered in a pair of cracks so that two twisted old trees could survive. And he had no tools to dig a grave anyway. Her own people could tend to her, of course, but he might go all the way to the Sault without meeting another soul. And he could get her in the boat now, but the added weight would be hideously dangerous. He stood up and walked to the west side of the rock, stepping between the two closely spaced trees. What he saw – the waves and the sky – finished the decision. He would have to leave at once, and the body would have to stay here.

He pulled her as near to the middle of the little piece of land as he could, and he wedged her between the cypress trunks. He glanced at the distance to the next island, and satisfied his conscience that no wolves would come here, not until the ice came, anyway. And when the bay did freeze, she'd already be entombed by the snow. She'd have to stay, and he'd have to get on into shelter himself quickly. There was no longer any doubt: it was a storm, for certain.

Stopping here had cost him almost three quarters of an hour. He launched his canoe and paddled carefully out from behind the rock. The waves met him with more strength than they'd had, the wind was sharper and heavy with the smell of snow. He picked his course and settled down to it, making each stroke carefully and deliberately, stabbing the paddle into the water, drawing back along the top rail, making the little outward curve at the end. He worked as hard at it as was wise, not as hard as he could. Exhausting himself would mean death; only keeping on at one solid pace would bring him into safety. He began to pray, reciting the Lord's Prayer (the only one he could remember all the way through).

"Pater noster, qui es in caelis," stroke. "Sanctificetur nomen tuum", stroke." Adveniat regnum tuum," stroke. "Fiat voluntas tua," stroke. "Sicut in caelo et in terra," stroke.

The words were just syllables to him. He spoke no Latin in the conscious sense. But he'd been taught to say these strange words, following along with his father or a priest, and they were the only means he knew for coercing fate. He corrected his path slightly so that the canoe pierced a larger wave more directly. He rode up and over it, felt a flush of adrenaline as the bow dipped almost to the water, and then angled back toward the dim island ahead.

" Panem nostrum quotidianum da nobis hodie," stroke. "Et dimitte nobis debita nostra sicut," stroke. "Et nos dimittimus debitoribus nostris," stroke.

Gaston's right arm began to cramp up. At the top of the next wave, the land ahead seemed no nearer.

"Et ne nos inducas in tentationem," stroke. "Sed libera nos a malo. Amen." stroke.

He took a deep breath and began again. "Pater noster ..." Over the noise of the wind he heard a shout. He didn't dare turn to look, but it came from behind. All he could do was to keep on paddling, keep the canoe pointed into the weather. Keep on praying. By the time he got to "lead us not", there was movement in his peripheral vision. Two strokes later, another canoe was coming up beside him, ranging on his weather side and easing the action of the waves. Two more strokes and Gaston could see that it was a larger boat, a *canot du nord,* and there were three Ojibwe men and a woman in it. All four were paddling. He realized that one of the men was an acquaintance, a man he'd traded with. There were shouts and gestures and pointing ahead, in the direction of the rabbit island. He allowed himself to ease the paddling slightly. The pain from his arm slacked off, and he realized suddenly that he'd been terrified. Now in company with other humans, he was merely tired, and instead of praying, he began running over his words in *Nishnaabemwin,* trying to piece together what he'd say about the body left behind on a tiny island.

In the end, they stopped one island short, landing on a beach on the lee side of a small piece of land, just barely separated from the larger one. There were few rabbits here, but no one was interested in hunting. Both boats carried travel food, and what seemed more important than hunting was simply starting a fire and securing the boats, turned on their sides as wind breaks. This was work every one of them had done many times before, and little talking was needed. When there was an outline of a camp with a fire and with shelter at least for people lying down, there was time to talk. The woman spoke good French, and the men spoke in their language slowly, with gestures. The dog they had with them said nothing at all. He got as close to the fire as he dared and went to sleep.

The people said their names and their recent history. Gaston explained as far as was necessary why he was being such a fool as to travel alone on the lake at this time of year. He named the man he was coming to see, and the Indians agreed that they'd seen him at the Sault, last week. They were coming back, they said, to the Sault from a last trip down into the bay. Gaston thanked them for travelling with him. That he'd been doing something dangerous and they'd probably saved him was obvious to all of them, and it was left quietly aside. The dog sighed and stretched.

"Now," Gaston said, "I have to ask you about someone." The others looked politely curious. "This was a woman, and I think she may have been what you call a two-spirit woman." The Ojibwe looked at each other. "She wore men's clothes. Her hair was like a man's."

There was a pause. "And she is dead," said Gaston. "Her body was floating in the water."

The man Gaston had met before said something to the woman. It was too fast for Gaston to understand. "What," the woman said, "happened to her?"

"She drowned," said Gaston. "I took her to a small island – a place with two trees only. I had to leave her there."

No one said anything for a long time. Finally the woman told him "She was an Iron Woman. She was always angry with this one man, and when he ... laughed ... *quel est le mot?* ... mocked at her, she went away. By herself. We were afraid she would do that. We were looking for her."

"I'm sorry," said Gaston, "that I couldn't bring her here."

"We'll go," said the woman. "After the storm or in the Spring."

"She'll be gone," said the oldest of the men. "She'll be in *Minawaanigoziwining* already. Even now. But we'll bring her here anyway." Again, people stared quietly into the fire. The dog twitched and growled in its sleep.

"Do you know how dogs came to us?" asked the woman. "A giant owned the first dog, and the dog could grow as big as it wanted to. Two of our people were lost and they were threatened by the *Windigo*, but the giant made the dog grow big and chase the spirit away. He sent the dog to take our people home. When they got there, the dog became small again. And he was friendly, and he let the people feed him. And that's how the Ojibwe came to have dogs."

"*Je n'ai jamais connu un chien qui refuse d'être nourri*," said Gaston. "What dog ever refused to be fed?"

Helarctas maylayanus The Sun Bear and *Ovis dalli* The Dall Sheep

Mac MacArthur rubbed his hands together, passing one over the other. They were cold, and they ached. Again and without wanting to, he asked himself "*Why do I live here?*" A fruitless, rhetorical question: he lived in Michigan, in this odd little city, because he did. You can't get much more existential than that, he thought. "*I'm here because I'm here, because I'm here, because I'm here ...*". Lyrics stuck with Mac, even if the name of the song sometimes didn't.

Where would he rather be? Another question he didn't really want to ask or answer, but when he did ask, the answer was never a concrete, extant location. It was a set of attributes, characteristics of his imaginary great good place. A Mediterranean climate, an island with a small native and expatriate population, speaking French or Italian with a bit of English on the side. Just enough tourists to provide entertainment. A cafe right across the street from a Bistro. Fresh fish straight off the boats. Slow traffic so that dogs could safely graze. High speed Internet. And world-class oncology. That last one ruined the picture and usually ended the daydream.

Here was, of course, Ann Arbor, the Athens of the West, home of the University of Michigan, home of deferred street maintenance policies that would rival the Penn Central Railroad. He owned a house in Ann Arbor. His wife's career was here, and his had been until he'd been blindsided by a "treatable but not curable" kind of cancer. He was here because he had friends here. Because (if you carefully stayed inside the surrounding ring of freeways) you didn't have to see too many big-box retail stores and supermarkets. It wasn't an entirely boring place in terms of terrain; thanks to glaciation and the Huron River there were some hills and valleys. This was in distinct contrast to the bulk of southeastern Michigan, which was flat as a pancake (if you can imagine a pancake covered with asphalt and chain restaurants).

Here was a community he knew and (he flattered himself) understood. He'd been a detective with the Ann Arbor police department for years. Even after he retired, there'd been a tacit and informal agreement; he'd occasionally provide some advice. Once in a while, he'd go somewhere and look around a crime scene. Sometimes, he'd go along on a interview, just to make sure all the questions were asked. Once, he'd been in a shootout while advising; another time, he'd helped arrest a homicide suspect (or more accurately, his dogs had helped.) Just last week, he'd been asked to observe and comment as a trio of young imbeciles were questioned about the choking death of an elderly man. None of this was anything but dabbling, but it kept him from going mad with boredom.

Another way to arms-length the sameness of retirement was to add little touches of eccentricity to his affect. Having established himself as a regular customer at a favorite coffee shop, he now began to expand the legend a bit, wearing his huge rabbit fur hat in the cold weather, and bringing along a pair of dogs in the passenger seats of his pickup, back and front. The young women who staffed the drive through knew him – how could they not? – and his regular order, coffee and a couple of dog biscuits.

The coffee place was a local chain, and Mac's neighborhood shop was in a small historic building on the corner (or something like a corner) where westbound Washtenaw veered off to the northwest, leaving two of its lanes to become Stadium and carry on straight west. The shop sat in the triangle, with entrances from Stadium and Washtenaw, and its building had been an early gas station, owned by the Tuomy family. It had a feudal feeling since it was built of brick and cut field stone. It was the only coffee shop Mac knew of that would be capable of withstanding a siege.

On this bitterly cold winter morning, Mac and his canines were preparing to drive off. The dogs had inhaled their snacks, and Mac was fumbling to get his wallet back into a pocket and secure his travel mug. It might be knocked over by the dogs, of course, but a more likely risk was simply dropping a tire into a pothole and slopping hot coffee and milk around. He got things sorted out and started to drive forward toward the exit onto Stadium. But as the truck began moving, both of the dogs pricked up their ears and focused sharply on something off to the east. In a second, Mac heard it, too, sirens, and their Doppler shift said they were approaching. The east-bound lane of Stadium was clear, and there was only a single delivery van, two blocks off, coming from the west. On a whim, Mac pulled out onto the street and turned immediately left into a strip mall parking lot. He swung around in a half circle and parked the truck in a space facing the road. It irked him that he'd become a gawker, but somehow the sound of the approaching sirens suggested more than just an ambulance. Like any reasonably good investigator, he was a curious animal.

So were his friends, the German Shepherds. One was an older female mix, shepherd and something else. Her name was Snacker. The other was a middle-aged, prematurely retired police dog. His long, official name had Gustav in it, and of course he was called Goose. Goose was now very interested in the police noises, and if Goose was interested in something, Snacker was too. Mac stepped out and walked around to the other side of the pickup.

It wasn't an ideal position from a tactical standpoint. With all the leaves off the trees, he could see as far as the actual split between Washtenaw and Stadium. If the pursuit (if that's what it was) turned away and headed off towards the University, he'd lose sight of the action at once, off behind the coffee shop and the little rise of ground it sat on. He'd see more of it if it stayed on Stadium, running off toward the west side of town. He dug out his smart phone and started the radio scanner application.

Fifteen minutes earlier and four and a half miles away, Rusty Cornley was nervous. He didn't like being out of familiar places, and this place looked different from home. It was cleaner, for one thing. The piles of snow weren't completely blackened, and the dumpsters, well, they were behind the stores, not out front. That wasn't normal.

Rusty was seventeen, and although he'd never had a diagnosis, he was probably somewhere well along the autism spectrum.

He'd never had a diagnosis because his parent was very cost-focused when it came to healthcare. Rusty was prone to injuries, minor ones, when he was younger. He'd fall and bruise himself, get little cuts and scrapes, even once a mild beating from another boy, and for those things, his mother would take him to Emergency. They'd patch him up and tell Mom to bring him back in a week. She never did, though, because those visits cost money. At Emergency, they'd treat you and if they did send a bill, you just didn't bother with it. It went away, eventually. And Mom's biggest concern was food and rent. If there was something wrong with Rusty that was less immediately obvious, she was certain that whatever the fix might be, she couldn't afford it. If her boy wasn't the brightest light on Broadway, it was up to the schools to fix that. If you went to school, you got smarter, or what was the point? When Rusty didn't really seem to benefit all that much from small town public education, she just added it to the list of ways in which the government had failed her. They couldn't keep the streets fixed and they couldn't teach the kids nothing.

The boy didn't precisely drop out of high school; as he grew up, he faded away, spending more and more days in his room or with his two or three friends. The biggest issue was when his mother made him go back and retrieve a coat he'd left in his locker. He went, sheepishly, since he hadn't been in the place for months, but of course he couldn't remember the combination. Mom had been mad, but somehow she'd made it right. He had the coat back. He was wearing it now, huddling into it, slid down in the driver's seat.

He and another boy had driven up here from a place south of Monroe, where he and Mom lived in a mobile home community. Telegraph Road ran from there almost straight northeast up toward Detroit, and then it suddenly bent due north and became the spine of the downriver cities. Taylor was the first of them, and it was a little more suburban, a little more prosperous than Monroe. The strip mall of small, one-off businesses where they stopped was just urban enough to make Rusty uncomfortable. His friend had said to wait, maybe even do the driving on the way home. He said he'd be gone just a few minutes.

Actually, he came back in even less time. He got in the passenger's side and banged the door.

"Closed! Dammit all to hell! Told me they'd be here! Son-a-bitch, we come all the way up here for nothin'." Rusty was alarmed. The other boy was a year older, more accomplished, in control of things, usually. If he was upset, Rusty was prepared to be, too. They'd come up here to sell some gold that his friend had. One of the shops did have a "We buy gold!" sign, but apparently they weren't buying it today.

"Come all the way up here for nothin'," his friend repeated. "Cost us for gas and all. You got any money?" Rusty said that he didn't. "We gotta get some money for gas, just to get home." He paused. "You up for going on a bit more?"

"Yeah, I guess," said Rusty.

"I know one more place we can try. Up in Ypsilanti." He pronounced it *Yips*-a-lanty. "Might be open. Hell, they gotta be. Can't make any money if they ain't." Rusty wasn't sure if he meant the shop or themselves, but either way, he hoped they'd be open. And so he agreed to go on, and he agreed to do some driving.

Rusty was physically able to drive a car. He had no driver's license, but he knew how to do it, how to keep from breaking too many laws, how to listen to directions. When he was coming up on sixteen, Mom had taken him out and around Monroe, mostly as a precursor to driver's ed. He never got around to that, but the enormity of driving without a license was never made clear to him. He seldom had anything to drive, anyway, and his friends weren't usually keen on anybody else driving their cars. But it was still morning, the bigger streets were clear of snow, and he made a good show of knowing what he was doing as his companion directed him west. He even got in a little freeway time when they hit I-94.

Now they were on surface streets again, heading out of Ypsilanti's city center, out along Washtenaw Avenue. After the residential neighborhood beyond the EMU campus, the scenery became more familiar. The dominant feature became strip malls of a certain age, gas stations, combination signs with five or six different businesses listed. Suddenly, the other boy told Rusty to turn left into a parking lot. He parked, as directed to, in front of a cell phone shop, an odd, eight-sided building with a concrete roof like an inverted umbrella. The sides were higher than the center, and presumably rain and melting snow got somehow channeled down inside the store and into the storm drains.

"That's where we're goin'," said his friend, pointing to another building off to the right. "They got a 'open' light on, anyhow." The other shop did have its lights on, and a somewhat vague name, with a subscript "Buy – Sell – Trade". "I'm goin' in ... you wanna wait?" Rusty said he would wait.

He sat there, staring ahead at the cell phone store. He could read in a utilitarian way, but it was mostly contextual. He knew what a gas station looked like, and therefore he understood what most of its signs said, since he knew what kinds of things gas stations sold. He could read road signs because if you were going to drive, you had to know what they meant. These signs, though, were almost unintelligible. They offered phone technologies and deals that were beyond his experience, and they were stated mostly in acronyms. His stomach reminded

23

him that it had been a while since breakfast, and that it was a long way back home for lunch.

As he sat there, wondering whether to leave the car on for heat or turn it off to save gas, the door of the cell phone shop banged open, and two young men stumbled out, tripping over the door sill. An older man was right behind them, and he grabbed one around the neck. The other fellow took off running, but the man and his quarry struggled in a confused way, right there in front of Rusty. The young man got an arm free and punched his adversary in the side of the head. He broke loose, but the man grabbed his coat as he tried to run. He broke away again and lunged straight onto the car's hood and into Rusty's face. There was a moment's pause. Nothing but the windshield separated Rusty from a frantic thug, desperate to get away from a botched shoplifting attempt. Rusty snapped. He dropped the car into gear and stomped on the gas pedal. He'd gotten it into drive, unfortunately, and it jumped forward twelve inches, the front wheels hitting the curb block at the end of the parking space. It came to a sudden stop, and the shoplifter was thrown forward off the hood and onto the sidewalk. The shop owner, bleeding from a cut on the side of his face, leapt onto him and began the process of beating him into unconsciousness.

Rusty dropped the car into reverse and backed up blind, not having enough psychological bandwidth to consider anything but getting away. Fortunately, there was nothing solid behind him; a bystander jumped out of the way, and Rusty continued backwards, out onto and across Washtenaw Avenue. He almost jumped the curb on the far side, braking just in time to come to a stop, perpendicular to traffic. He jammed the shifter back into drive and turned without a thought of any kind, dodging other cars and yelling unintentional words. He found himself heading out of Ypsilanti at forty-five miles an hour, headed for Ann Arbor.

Within seconds, three separate people had dialed 911, and the synthesis of the intelligence received was that someone was being assaulted and had maybe been hit by a car in the course of robbing a cell phone place. There might have been two or three people involved, and some of them were escaping in a car. No one thought to get a license plate number. Nobody was sure what kind of car, although one person said it was old and kind of black. Someone else said blue. In some mysterious way, the information that actually reached police officers suggested that there might have been a gun involved. Later on, no one could determine where that idea originated, but at least half the officers who responded said they believed somebody was armed.

Rusty had no gun, of course. He had no idea where he was and no idea where he was going. He was operating almost completely on instinct. He was somewhere he shouldn't be, something really bad had happened, Mom would be furious. All he could do was drive as fast as traffic would let him and wait for a sign, one that he could read. A big green sign saying "HOME" would be good.

He didn't even make it as far as Hewett Road before there was a police car behind him. An Eastern Michigan University officer had heard the radio traffic and then, almost at once, spotted Rusty weaving from lane to lane. She got in behind him and turned on her lights, but Rusty didn't stop; he didn't even notice her, in fact. His whole focus was on the road ahead. She made the call, and the dispatcher told her to stay in contact and wait for more officers. Later, when the recorded transmissions were examined, this one still didn't say the word "*gun*" or even "*armed*", but a garbled portion of it could have been understood as "*dangerous*". Other officers certainly heard the call, and this might have been the thing that lead to misunderstandings. Wherever the idea began, the notion spread; there was a high speed chase in progress, involving

25

flight from an armed robbery. It was remarkably similar to a mob chasing someone down an alley and shouting "Stop thief!"

When police agencies select pursuit tactics, they have to make assumptions about the subject's intentions. Is he trying to outrun the law or hide from it? In the first case, he'll try to distance himself from the crime, going fast on major streets or highways. If he wants to hide, he'll take sudden turns, reverse course, slip into residential areas. He may look for a place to abandon his vehicle and run. In Rusty's case, he seemed to be fleeing, and it was a fair bet that he'd look for a freeway. Going the way he was going, the nearest opportunity would be the Washtenaw entrances to M-23, right on the edge of Ann Arbor. The Ypsilanti city officers and one car from Ypsi Township stayed behind him, and the Washtenaw County Deputies and the State Police were asked to try stopping him at those ramps, one going north and one (the more likely one) going south. As it turned out, the County had only one unit they could send, but the State Troopers had just cleared an accident at I-94, and they were able to commit a car and an SUV. On the chance that the subject didn't try for the highway, Ann Arbor was tasked with stopping him as he went on west.

Rusty wasn't thinking along these lines at all. He'd never heard of M-23 and wasn't looking for it. He wanted to be home and away from all this. He could now see the police cars behind, and he noted the Township car blocking the left turn he wasn't planning to make onto Golfside. He squirmed through the traffic at the intersection, using the left turn lane and running the red light. The street emptied ahead, and he sped up, running through a mix of abandoned or doomed businesses, paired with new chain restaurants and tanning salons. It looked like home, but it wasn't. There was too much grass showing through the snow, even a few deliberately-planted trees. And the farther he went, the more trees there were, especially on the left. Even now, with all the branches bare, trees made him nervous. Home was a place without trees, and the more trees there were, the farther from home he seemed to be.

He would have been more nervous if he'd known that a set of ugly, bare buildings on the right was the Washtenaw County Service Center, including the Sheriff's department and the jail. He didn't know that, and he didn't know that just ahead a Deputy who'd come out of the Center was laying spike strips across the northbound entrance ramp to M-23. Rusty was nearing the old-style cloverleaf interchange with the highway and closing in on the most accident-prone intersection in the county, where Washtenaw Avenue and Carpenter Road come together and blend with traffic getting on and off the freeway. Traffic had vanished, now, though, because it was blocked off. Here was where the authorities planned to stop him. The State Police SUV had gone off-roading a bit in order to block the southbound ramp. The cruiser was waiting to go after him if he hit the spikes and went on north. It was a sound plan, but it didn't take into account that Rusty had no plan of his own.

He drove relentlessly straight, under the freeway and up the slight rise past an older shopping center, a couple of tire stores, and a roadhouse Italian restaurant. The road dropped downhill and into a newer, glossier commercial area; ahead was one of the largest intersections in the city, a choke point where six lanes of Huron Parkway crossed five lanes of Washtenaw. The Ann Arbor police hadn't gotten things closed down yet, and there was still traffic. Rusty saw an opening; a car in the right lane was smart enough to turn on red and get out of the way, and he veered into the space created. An Ann Arbor patrol car came up from the south just at that moment, saw the lights from the cars behind Rusty, and made a snap decision to get ahead of him. He went left onto Washtenaw with lights and sirens going.

Hee-Sun Park had been in the US for less than a month. She'd come with her husband , since he was going to get his Masters from the university. She had never been out of South Korea before, didn't have a license to drive, and certainly didn't want to; she was learning the bus system. Today, she'd walked down the Parkway sidewalk toward the bus stop, and as she reached the intersection, she heard the sirens. In a second, she saw a police car make a fast turn and go off toward the city. She turned her head to watch him, curious as anyone would be. She was still looking the wrong way when Rusty's front wheels slipped on packed snow, and she never saw his car when it jumped the curve and knocked her halfway across the Parkway. Witnesses said that she was completely off the ground for at least ten feet.

There was nothing else in Rusty's way, nothing except Hee-Sun. He missed light poles, crossing signals, and a car that just slipped past in front of him. The front end of his car was in bad shape, but the wheels were still turning and somehow he kept going. Now he was sobbing wildly, hyperventilating, nearly paralyzed with fear. Traffic might have stopped him; it had backed up at a new light near the top of the next hill, but it changed and at least some of the drivers were alert enough to see the lights coming up behind them. They scattered like squirrels, some going ahead, some stopping, some pulling over. One turned left in front of an oncoming truck and lost his rear bumper as the truck scraped by. Rusty breasted the hill, looked ahead, and saw another of the shallow valleys that bound the city on its east side. The road went down slightly, up slightly, and at the crown there was yet another light. But in between, the left lane was empty. He pointed the car and accelerated.

There's no way of saying how long he would have lasted, running mindlessly west into town. Eventually, the road he was using would have bent almost ninety degrees north and steered him into the peripheral shopping areas along the west side. There was a freeway interchange out there, too, giving him a chance to get on I-94 if he could recognize the opportunity. But the old sedan didn't live that long. Just as Rusty came to that Y intersection, just as he passed Mac's coffee shop, he stuck the left front wheel into a pile of hard, frozen snow, shoved into a small mountain by the plows. It wrenched the wheel sideways, and the tie rod broke. The car spun left, sliding on the last half-inch of ice left on the street, went around almost three hundred and sixty degrees, crossed the opposing lane, flew across a sidewalk, and came up hard against a curb in the parking lot where MacArthur was standing.

As Rusty's car came flying into the lot, Mac stepped involuntarily back, bumped into the side of his truck, lost his footing on the snow, and sat down hard. As he struggled back to his feet, his first impression was of loud barking. Whether because of the crash or because they thought Mac was hurt, the dogs were freaking out. Goose was scrabbling at the window sill from the back seat of the extended cab. Mac usually put a window down slightly when he left the dogs in the car, and Snacker was in the front seat , with an inch of nose out the crack, howling threats at the world. Mac stood up, took a look at the wreck, and was immediately confronted with a choice, specifically a choice of pockets.

In the left breast pocket of his coat was a retiree badge, on the same lanyard as his concealed-carry license. In the left lower pocket were his keys, including the key to a lockbox in the bed of the truck; there would be first aid gear in there. And in his right lower pocket there was a small handgun. His phone was already occupying his left hand, since he'd been listening to the scanner, and so he had to choose what to do with the right: identify himself, help the driver of the crashed car, or step into a potential gunfight. He'd heard the chatter about an armed subject.

Before he could make up his mind, two things happened. First, Rusty opened the driver's side door and climbed out. He'd banged his forehead on the steering wheel, and he was bleeding slightly. He and Mac made eye contact at a distance of perhaps fifteen feet. Weeping, babbling, and bleeding, Rusty started walking toward Mac. Mac unsnapped his lower right pocket and stuck his hand in.

The second thing was the arrival of an Ann Arbor patrol car, making a sliding turn off Washtenaw onto Stadium and driving straight into the parking lot. It was a car driven by Officer Jeri Klein, a woman Mac knew. She, however, knew next to nothing about this situation; she'd heard the radio traffic, and she knew that somebody who might be armed was fleeing from the cops. As she jumped out of her car, she saw a wreck, an injured man, and (*"What?"*) that old, retired Detective with his pack of pet wolves.

"Oh, for Christ's sake ... Stop!" she yelled, more or less at Rusty. Whatever the situation was, the important thing was for everybody to stop whatever it was they thought they were doing. "Get down on the ground! Get down, you hear me?!" Rusty didn't even glance at her; he took another uncertain step toward Mac. Mac's hand closed around the butt of his pistol.

There was another snow-crunching noise, and a second patrol car came over the curb and onto the sidewalk. Officer Mark Fraser had heard the radio traffic while on Main Street, and he'd come out east on Stadium, nearly losing it on the new bridge. Now he arrived on the scene with a certain amount of panache. As he got out of the car, he was only five feet or so from Rusty. He joined the chorus of shouted commands and loud barking, and unlike Jeri, was in a position to see that

Rusty's hands were empty. Instead of drawing a weapon, he charged in and knocked the boy down. Jeri bolted the last couple of yards and as Fraser was trying to get the handcuffs on, she came down hard with her knee on the small of Rusty's back. Mac took his hand out of his pocket and snapped the flap again.

Fifty-plus miles to the east, a woman rolled over in bed. The light coming through the drapes was feeble, but it was light. Morning. "*What time is it?*" she thought. She should have heard her husband's alarm clock by now. She reached out for her own clock and pressed a button. The display lit up, reading eight thirty-five. Gerald must have forgotten to set his. She rolled back the other way and said "Gerald. It's late." There was no reply. "Gerald!" she repeated. Another roll the other way, and she fumbled with the lamp on her nightstand. She raised herself on one elbow.

The other bed was unoccupied, still made up, still just as it had been when she went to bed the night before. She always went to bed before Gerald did, sometimes even before he got home. But last night, he'd been home, sitting in his office. She'd said "Good night," formally, as she went upstairs. He'd waved a hand, absently.

Ten minutes after that, the emergency dispatcher at the Grosse Pointe Park Department of Public Safety took its first call of the morning.

Mustela nivalis The Least Weasel

Fisher Gerald Temple. He turned it over in his imagination, trying again to come to terms with his name. To anyone he knew, from his wife to people he worked with, he was Gerald. A few new acquaintances had tried to make it Gerry, but he discouraged it. For a while in college, he'd abbreviated the first name, becoming F. Gerald. He'd even toyed with the initials, trying to get away with just FGT. Neither of those stuck, and both sounded pompous, especially in dating situations. Finally, he gave up and used Gerald alone as a social name and all three for formal things like job applications, his resume, and his business cards. And now he had to accept a new version. There was a character limit on the door signs at his new job, and without asking, the office manager had ordered him a wood grain-laminate tag that said "Fisher Temple".

"*I wish I had a frosted glass door,*" he thought. "*With the name painted on it. I could read it backward, like Nick Danger: ELPMET REHSIF.*" He'd tried that reference, tentatively, on the HR executive, but if Gerald was nearly too young to remember the Firesign Theater, she was absolutely so. She gave him the "*I wonder if we've made a mistake here?*" look, and he set aside humor in the workplace. FastFF was not that kind of company, apparently.

Gerald's background was financial and conservative, but his personality had trouble staying within that mold. He was born in a suburb of Hartford, and he was pushed toward some kind of middle job in the world of numbers. No one picked him for a billionaire, but he was expected to follow a path, wear a suit, get a business degree, and move into a career much like his father's. Both his parents were severe people, not dour in a protestant New Englander sense, but conventional and frightened by imagination. They were much farther up scale than their parents had been, and not all of their combined brothers and sisters had done as much. There was an uncle who drove trucks and an aunt who was a musician. No matter how good a trucker one was or how brilliant a cellist, the Temple family didn't consider those qualifications to be success. Several generations of Gerald's family had been Catholics, and he grew up with it, never considering it

32

something to choose or to see beyond. The equation remained: success equals respectability equals success.

And so he got out of high school without much in the way of stains. He didn't like beer or the rubbish that high school students think is beer. No one offered him any drugs. There were a few equally respectable girls in the class, and he did manage to have dates for the milestone events, but he was one of the last, shrinking set of American teens who had trouble imagining their parents having sex. Sex was frightening, in fact, and he and his dates didn't do much more than dance awkwardly; after the prom, there was a quick, equally awkward kiss. He went off to college a virgin, and he got the mandated finance degree. He met a few people, but none of them managed to corrupt him. They didn't really try; why would they?

He accepted his parents' lukewarm and flat-sounding congratulations, and through his father and his father's colleagues, he got an entry level job at an insurance company. Suddenly, a weight of responsibility lifted. For the first time in years, success wasn't up to him. All he had to do now was show up, dress appropriately, and do simple things. Check a financial filing against published and well-known standards. Ensure that section A was consistent with what appeared in section Y. Check that the basis for an estimate was documented; whether it was a reasonable estimate was not his concern. A large portion of his mind was abruptly freed up for other topics.

One of them, predictably, was a set of steps to cover the future. He put money into very conservative stock funds and a bit more into bonds. He observed people at higher levels in the company, and he made a list of skills and behaviors to learn so that he would be promotable. But outside the office, sitting alone in his apartment, he began to read.

At first, he read worthless things, consumer magazines, apocalyptic science fiction, "Christian" novels. He bought these things, read them, and threw them away. It hadn't occurred to him to keep them, anymore than he'd want to keep the packaging from takeout food. He allowed himself an hour of television a night, almost always network news programs, then he'd read the latest fluff until he was tired of it, carefully make sure everything was shut off, closed up, and locked, and go to bed.

He lived this way for almost two years. He saw his parents at intervals and went occasionally to Church events. At one of those events, he saw a flier on the lobby bulletin board, promoting the local library. His diet of unchallenging reading was becoming unpleasant, and he had an idea that libraries were somehow governmental, that they were vaguely official, and that their contents were like raw ingredients. His neighborhood was gentrifying rapidly, and he was being exposed to foodies and organic things, ideas that seemed to value basics over processing. Even his boss talked enthusiastically about cooking. Gerald did no cooking himself. He ate chain restaurant food and takeout food, and his shopping was for breakfast cereal and laundry soap. But he mingled the notions of culinary basics and from-scratch cooking with the idea of roots and foundations in what he read. "*Maybe*," he thought, "*I should try something ... older*." Instead of his usual stop at a Barnes and Noble, he dropped into the library.

He'd been in university libraries repeatedly, of course, but this was different. There were children, for one thing. There were older people, some of them using computers, some wearing headphones. The young woman at the front desk was besieged by a group of middle school students, frantic to get at assigned books, glance through them, and get back outside. This was the second frustrating and unpleasant thing that the young woman had dealt with in the last hour. The other was a sarcastic message from a boyfriend. And most unfortunately, he and Gerald looked much the same.

When he got her attention, she was rather short with him. He was looking for advice, and she was only prepared to give directions. "Foundation reading?" she said. "Foundations of what field?"

"Well, I guess ..."

"Do you want philosophy? That's the one hundreds. Over there." She pointed.

Philosophy didn't sound like the thing Gerald wanted. "I think, more like the foundations of literature", he said.

"American literature?"

Gerald neither spoke nor read anything other than English. "Yes."

"Okay, the other side of the stacks. The eight-tens."

"Um, yes. Do you have a ... Do you recommend anything?" A pause. The librarian looked closely at him for the first time. He did look like that bastard she'd been seeing. But dumber. More insensitive. Wearing a suit, for Christ's sake.

"Sure," she said. "How about a feel-good novel?"

"Oh, great. Yes, please," said Gerald.

"Try this, then." She tore off a piece of note paper and printed clearly. "*John Dos Passos; The 42nd Parallel*".

Heroin, opiates, and opioids begin slowly. The mind begins to want them before the body does. Crack is much quicker. For

Gerald, the work of John Dos Passos was like crack. From the first page of *The 42nd Parallel*, he was stunned, addicted, swept up. *"It was the speech that clung to the ears, the link that tingled in the blood: U.S.A"*. Every paragraph mentioned something new, something he'd never heard of, sometimes a phrase or a name or an occupation that he did know but he'd never understood. He read page after page of shifting rhythms, quoted song lyrics, The Camera Eye sections that reveal themselves as autobiographic; *"What is this?"* he asked himself, again and again. Finally, after the third evening sitting up until two o'clock, he grasped at a straw. *"It's writing. That's what it is. Writing."*

That hardpoint was his crutch. It let him slow down a bit and become slightly more comfortable with the flood of unfamiliar references. He began to keep a notebook next to him on the couch, and he used it to list things to look up. He looked up Eugene Debs and the Battle of Port Arthur. Big Bill Haywood and Luther Burbank. And Minor Keith. And Jean Jaurès. And Robert Lafollette. And the Sedition Act. When he finished reading the online biographies and the summary histories, he stopped for a whole week. He got his breath back, mentally. He'd consumed in one sitting a whole bottle of socialism and internationalism, aged but unmellowed. And he asked himself *"How do I feel about it?"* And *"Who am I, anyway?"* He didn't come up with a concrete answer, but he did feel slightly ashamed.

Equus asinus x Equus caballus The Mule

Frozen into her berth at Cleveland, the Waubuno was a quiet ship. The bridge was empty and crusted outside with snow. Her engines were cold, and the only power came from dockside connections. A hibernating bear still breathes, and his heart still beats; the Waubuno lay virtually dead. She waited as she had every winter since her launch, every year since 1943.

Until the ice let go of the Great Lakes, she was a dormant vessel, at the mercy of the weather. Other boats might get away, but she was trapped by her length in the upper lakes; she was too long for the locks on the Welland Canal, unable to get around Niagara and go down the Saint Lawrence to the sea. From Buffalo through Erie, up the Saint Clair to lake Huron, through the straits to Chicago or up the Saint Mary's to Superior, then west to Duluth or Thunder Bay, her long, useful life was bounded by the inland waters and their ice packs.

Now the winter had barely begun, and the Waubuno sat silently, brooding on the face of the waters.

Mustela nigripes The Black-footed Ferret

The gate attendant smiled and waved his hand at a three-year-old Mercedes. He knew the car and the driver. When he'd been hired to sit in this booth outside a set of condos, his boss had impressed on him the need to change attitude and behavior depending on who was driving in. The important people, the ones who were responsible for there being an attendant job at all, were the residents. Among the residents, there were three or four who'd pressed the condo association to hire a certain security company, theirs, and therefore they were even more important. Mr. Bauer was one of those important people, and he and his car and his usual times of coming and going were to be kept in mind.

To make it all easier, there was a cheat sheet with names and condo numbers and phone contact information. Mr. Bauer's entries also noted that he lived alone, had only one car, and had a housekeeper who came in during the day; she was almost never there when he was. Except for her, no one was expected on a regular basis. Mail went into the joint mail boxes outside the gate; deliveries were held at the gate itself. The housekeeper was authorized to pick up either one. Mr. Bauer's emergency contact was a phone number with the note "(admin)". Any visitors had to be authorized ahead of time; those who weren't had to wait while the attendant called for permission to enter.

Bauer seldom had visitors of either kind. He did business in the office or over lunch or on the phone in the evening. He was somewhere in his fifties, with thin gray hair wrapped around from ear to ear and nothing much on top. His eyebrows were darker and his black eyes slightly sunken. There were deep lines on either side of his nose, and the nose itself was rounded off; no point, no bulge. He wore no facial hair except a silvery stubble that was already showing up by 5:30, obvious by 6:00. His cheeks hadn't yet fallen into jowls, but it was clearly not far off. You might look at him and imagine any kind of a northern European background, from Dublin to Kiev; in fact, his parents and grandparents were German. His given name was Gudrun, but as a short, feisty, competitive child, he'd been fond of saying that he was "nobody's mark". So naturally, people called him Mark. When he started applying for jobs, he used it, and it stuck. He introduced himself by extending a large right hand and saying "Yeah, hi. I'm Mark Bauer."

Mark meant to spend this evening in the same way he did most of them. He'd heat up the meal that Karla, his housekeeper and second cousin, had left for him in the refrigerator. He'd have one glass of wine with it, then one ounce, never any more, of bourbon to sip while he watched television. His TV wasn't for entertainment; he deliberately flipped around among the lower-brow cable channels, looking for competitive intelligence. He ignored the programs and consumer product ads, movie trailers, buffet restaurant spots; his focus was on any kind of financial services being pitched to the poor and stupid.

There were no degrees or credentials after his name. He'd started on a business education, but after two years, he reasoned with himself: he could waste more time finding out what the rules are or get started and fly under the radar until he could hire people who knew exactly what was legal and what wasn't. So he began with small companies and sole proprietorships. He married and divorced, something so predictable that it seems almost unnecessary to mention. He was charged once with failing to report income, and he got out of it with a fine and restitution. He did a number of things without a license – contracting, for example – and other things without really having the money that he said he had. When the housing boom began, he dug into it and wrote some of the more worthless paper. He made a real company out of that, and had an office, employees, and so on. Being aware of how shaky the whole thing was, benefiting from being the boss, without superiors or a board, he could also see more easily than others when it began to fall apart, and he could make the decision to close the doors, lay everybody off, sell the copy machine and the file cabinets, and tiptoe away. Looking back, he called those days the screwing of the rich and dumb.

After the bubble popped, he kept his head down and looked for the next opportunity. He had a planning technique, not grandiose enough to be called strategic, but longer-sighted than merely tactical. He thought about supply and demand; if the old game was to take advantage of a lot of bozos with lots of money, what's changed? There aren't as many rich idiots anymore, but ... there are more and more poor ones! And so he made the next logical leap. Instead of a few raw deals with a large payoff, he'd find ways to skim a few dollars each from a lot of small, individual screwings.

He looked at the needs of his market; the disadvantaged needed survival money, wanted flash money, and thought they wanted respectable money. And so he eased himself into payday loans, buyouts, and debit cards. Only the loans were risky, and rapacious interest rates covered you there; the other two were guaranteed. An annuity buyout on your terms ensured on-going revenue at a greater rate than you paid (and you could always sell it on and take the cash yourself). And debit cards? Take somebody's money, charge them when they use it, and by definition prevent them from over running their balance. And (he smiled when he thought of it) all of that was the legal part.

He started the businesses from his home. Five years on, it was in an office with an Ann Arbor address. It had twenty-eight employees, a CEO (himself), a CFO with whom he saw eye to eye, and a combined COO, Corporate Council, and Human Resources executive. There were a couple of managers, called "Directors" to make their business cards look better, and two rooms of telephone staff. Everyone below the executives worked on the company's despicable but legal enterprises. Within the inner circle, Mark and his two colleagues operated a number of other efforts. They were absolutely not legal. Between the three of them, a term had evolved: "knowing". If you were aware of these additional lines of business, you "knew". Otherwise, you "didn't know".

The name of the company (the visible company at least, the one whose name was on the building) had originally been an afterthought as the papers were being signed. Bauer and the CFO came up with Fast Funding and Finance, and they let it go at that. It lasted a year, while they were building up the business, but when they starting talking to a consultant about some TV ads, she pushed them to rename it before they went public with the promotions. Bauer had to keep yanking on the reins, since the media person had visions of grandeur and portfolio material, conflicting with his vision of spending as little as possible. But they settled on a new name, FastFF, and a pitchman approach to the ads. "No humor", he insisted. "I don't want none of that talking lizard stuff. I can't stand that insurance lady with the white pants." And later on, he made it clear: "No singing!" Instead, they got a local actor with executive hair and his own suit. They named the character Fredrick Franklin ("It's FF, see, and Franklin sounds like money"), and FastFF began hitting the low-cost cable channels.

The Swift Fox and the Sun Bear

MacArthur hadn't had his coffee yet. It was an appointment morning, half a day every few months dedicated to the worship of Asclepius. He liked to schedule them in the morning, but it meant that he didn't often get to stop at the coffee drive-through. Instead, he'd park in an annoying structure on the University's annoying medical campus. He'd share a waiting room with unhappy children, all in a state of fear because they'd had their blood drawn here before, probably not as often as Mac, but enough to hate it. The screams and crying from the exam rooms didn't help. Once Mac had given up a few milliliters of his own blood, and after the obligatory chatter with the technician about the weather or the traffic, he'd move on, either to the next appointment or to wait in one of the public spaces. Showing up early did no good at all.

After he'd seen the oncologist or a Physician's Assistant, and after the last question was asked and answered ("How do you feel?" "Like hell." "Can you be more specific?" "No. Sorry."), Mac walked the long corridor trail back from the Cancer Center, through Taubman, down one floor, and finally out the front door of Mott. He retrieved his truck from the parking ramp, paid his fifty cents, and escaped. He'd be a bit ahead of time, but now that would be all right. He was headed for lunch, a window seat if he could get it, and an update from Jenn Langton.

They chose the Old Town Tavern, one of the few places with "old" legitimately in its name. Other store fronts on West Liberty had been bars on and off, but the Old Town claimed to have been a tap non-stop for nearly a hundred and twenty years. True, it hadn't had the same ownership all that time, but it was consistently a watering hole, a joint, a pub. Even during prohibition, it had somehow carried on. Inside, it was a long rectangular space with a clean sweep from the door to the kitchen wall. The bar itself ran along the right side; there were booths and a few tables in front, more tables in the back, and a giant oil painting of a nude woman. That it still had a stamped tin ceiling went without saying. Against the front wall, there were two window booths, looking out onto Liberty and Ashley, and Mac took one. He ordered water and against his better judgment, a cup of coffee.

He was a quarter of an hour early, and he used the time to make sure his notes from the oncologist were clear. There was nothing out of the ordinary, just adjustment of medications, a new appointment for imaging, setting up another test of his lungs. He was still making calendar entries when Jenn arrived.

"So you survived it, anyway," she said.

"Yeah, well, opinions differ."

Jenn glanced at his cup. "How's the, um, coffee?"

"Every bit as good as always." He sipped, made a face, and set it back down. Thin, pale brown, with a slick of oil and the burnt aroma of *rustica*. It was already cold. For bar coffee, it wasn't bad.

"Before you congratulate me," said Jenn, "Let me be the first to congratulate you."

"On what?"

"Well, apparently you and I have been having an affair. I hadn't noticed, myself. How about you?"

Mac blinked. "Explain."

"I've been spending a lot of time with Louie Burke, turning things over to him."

"Burke?", said Mac. "You're turning over to him?"

"He has the least on his plate. To be more accurate, I've been spending a lot of time *listening* to him, trying to get him to shut up long enough to hear what I'm telling him."

"Yeah," said Mac. "I can imagine that."

"Along the way, he was babbling about what Douglas said about me leaving and so on." Douglas was a Sergeant in charge of detectives. "Burke asked if he was surprised I was going, and Douglas said that didn't surprise him as much as me getting married."

"Why did that surprise him?"

"According to Burke, Douglas thought you and I were carrying on."

Mac closed his eyes for a second. "Well, well," he said. "You know, this puts me in an awkward position."

"How so? "

"Well, if I laugh, or if I say anything about how absurd that is, you'd have some right to take offense. I mean, it's kind of a do-these-pants-make-me-look-fat thing."

Jenn did laugh at that. Besides the twenty years difference in their ages and Mac's marriage, for her an affair with him would have been like sleeping with an uncle or an older brother. But she hadn't wanted to be the one to say "With Mac? That's ridiculous!" In fact, all she did say to Burke had been an icy "Obviously not." Now, she just said "I told Burke I didn't go for younger guys."

"Did you tell Andy that?" Andy Patel was younger than Jenn.

"I told him what Burke said. I asked him to put off challenging you to a duel until after the wedding."

"Because I'm such a good shot?" Jenn had empirical, first-hand knowledge that Mac couldn't hit the broad side of a barn, at least in a combat situation.

"Well, if you don't shoot him until after we're married, it'll make probating his estate easier."

Here, the waitress showed up. They ordered things; the bar menu was predictable and didn't require a lot of thought: a sandwich, a burger, just water, a polite refusal to have more coffee. It took a couple of minutes in all. Mac said "How badly is Burke going to drop the ball?"

"Badly, I guess," Jenn said. "He is, after all, a moron." She paused. "And I don't think I really care."

"I suppose not. But there's a problem with that."

"What?"

"You're a customer now, right? The department protects you, hypothetically."

"Because I'll be a civilian?"

"Like the rest of us."

"So ...?"

"So nothing. Except you probably do need to care how well he does. Self-preservation, if nothing else."

"When somebody breaks into my office or steals paperclips, I'll have to call the AAPD."

"And surprise, surprise, Louie Burke is the one who shows up to work on it."

"Oh, Lord."

They exhausted the rest of that topic as a dialogue, and it turned into a narrative. Jenn explained what she'd really be doing at her new job. Stolen paperclips might not be in her hands, but a break-in, absolutely. Background checks. Setting up a controlled area, getting it certified, keeping people from bringing cell phones into it. Security guards. Hiring a manager of information security. A lot of things she hadn't done before. She opened her mouth to say something else and then shut it again.

"Dammit, MacArthur," she said.

"What?"

"Don't you ever stop? Interrogating people, I mean?"

"Me?" Mac opened his eyes wide.

"It would never occur to you to just say *Tell me about the job.* "

"You have learned well, my child," said Mac. "Forget not what Rogers Sensei teaches us: '*Never miss a good chance to shut up*'. Especially since I assume you'll be getting a clearance."

"That's right. I will. Andy told me about that process."

"But while I'm gathering intelligence," said Mac, "I do have a couple of straight up questions for you."

"Okay, shoot."

"Is there a date for the wedding? Colleen wants to be sure she's not out of town."

"Soon. I mean, we'll have the date soon. Probably by next week." Mac knew the general plan already: a small gathering with a judge, very secular, very informal. Then some kind of reception / party afterward, somewhere. Preferably in Ann Arbor.

"The other thing: what's the word about that kid they arrested? The one who hit a ped on Washtenaw? Nearly hit me, for that matter."

Jenn frowned. "You were there, weren't you?"

"Yeah. And I'm apparently a witness. Nobody's saying anything. But I hear his mother's suing."

"Yes. Yes, she is. Look, Mac, I'm almost off to the world of serious secrets. I suppose I should practice saying *I can't discuss that* or something. But in confidence, yes, Mom is claiming unnecessary force."

"Bullshit."

"Well ... probably."

Mac looked over his glasses. "Probably?"

"He's got a ruptured spleen. And the ER docs said the crash into the parking lot wasn't likely to give him one."

"But I saw the arrest," Mac said. "Nobody beat on him. That patrol guy, Fraser? He came in and tackled him, got him around the knees. He went down on his front. And then Jeri Klein ..." Mac stopped.

"What?"

"You aren't so bad at this, either. Klein ran in and assisted in the arrest."

"She assisted in the arrest? It's being said that she knee-dropped him."

Mac thought about Jeri Klein. Tall with a north-west African face, a sharp nose, high cheek bones. No accent of any kind, and not a very outgoing way of meeting the world. A friend of his who'd been in the Army in the seventies had a word for squared-away, by-the-book, sharply-pressed-uniform types: "strack". Klein was strack.

"Last year," Jenn said, "she chased down a burglar over in studentville. He threw a punch, and she broke his nose, kneed him in the groin, and generally put him out of action."

"I remember that."

"It wasn't a problem. Other officers saw him start it. Nobody claimed anything."

"But ... ?" said Mac.

"That's all I've heard. There's just a sense around the office that maybe she's a little enthusiastic."

Both parties made strong eye contact. Mac's face lost all expression. "I didn't observe anything outside department procedure." He smiled. "You really *are* good at this."

"Useless now," Jenn said. "Except for interviewing job candidates." She put some money on the table. "I need to go. I need business shoes. Cop shoes aren't really business attire. She paused. "And Mac ..."

"Yeah?"

"I'd practice that line. It sounded a little flat."

Amorphochilus schnablii TheSmoky Bat

"*Always the same crap,*" DeLeon thought, "*Always the same damn thing!*" He slowed for the first turn of his commute, slipped sideways a bit, and ignored the horn of a northbound car. "Plenty of damn room, asshole," he said out loud. "*I'm late, I'm tryin' to get out of the house, and she's got to wait 'til then to lay more school crap on me!*" He was not happy, not at all. His commute wasn't too long in terms of miles, but it was often infuriating. It seemed to him that every idiot in the suburbs was trying to get into Ann Arbor at the same time he needed to. That he was one of those idiots himself didn't occur to him. Add poorly maintained streets, a couple of overloaded freeways, and four or five different sets of radar traps, and the trip made his stomach a sauce pan of extra acid. Throw in a surprise announcement from his wife about yet another problem between the daughter and her math teacher, and his mood reached something close to rage. "*She knew about that crap last night! She waited 'til I was almost out the damn door to drop it on me!*"

DeLeon Harper had more than enough crap to deal with on the job. He was the CEO of Mark Bauer's FastFF, and he was the one who got to figure out the ways and means for each of Bauer's little ideas. He was younger than Bauer and he believed he was smarter, too. But besides a C-level salary and a great deal more in money that never appeared on a W-2, he had another strong incentive to perform well. If he didn't, it wouldn't be Mark Bauer alone who went to jail. Harper was the one who kept the company out of trouble; Bauer had made sure of that. Once in a while, it occurred to Harper that being a little smarter in his choice of jobs might have been a good thing.

Today, he was late and mad, and there were things he had to get done, few of them pleasant. To ease the pain of a day in the office, some people stopped off for coffee or treats on their way in. His way of rewarding himself for getting out of bed was more fundamental: he drove aggressively. And in reasonable weather, he had the car for it. He was no luxury car guy, not a Lexus or BMW fan,, not interested in Lamborghinis. No, he'd treated himself to a new Dodge Charger, black, and with no weenie V6, either. His executive ride packed the full-on six-and-a-half liter V8. The only problem was, Harper lived in a place where unreasonable weather was frequent. The Charger's ludicrously powerful drive train began in the front of the car and ended in the rear; all the torque went straight to the rear wheels. With normal tires and a half inch of snow, it was functionally immobile. It would simply sit there and spin. They told him that as he drove it off the lot. "You know, this ain't really a winter car." After the first snow fall, he'd been forced to agree and go get a set of winter tires.

This morning, his drive south to the freeway was slow and frustrating. He made his turn onto Ford Road, and went up and over tracks and an industrial park. Most mornings, when he crested the bridge, he'd be able to see the freeway entrance a mile ahead. His game was to see how quickly he could get there, how many slow vehicles he could pass in order to be ahead of them before the two hundred and seventy degree ramp to 275. The worse the traffic was, the more he enjoyed the challenge.

Half way there, the industrial landscape turned to big box stores. He had two traffic lanes to work with plus a left turn lane and multiple right side turnouts. He was averaging fifty miles an hour, cutting it close on yellow lights and doing a questionable left-right around a semi. The rear end gave him a slight warning as he cut back in, slipping right and scaring the truck driver enough to make him brake and tap the air horn. Harper ignored both the horn and the skid. He knew just enough about driving to come off the gas, and the car straightened up. The overpass loomed up; his entrance was on the other side, around one lobe of a classic cloverleaf. To get the maximum fun out of it, he needed to be set up in the right lane, ready to slip onto the turnout. He braked for a mini-van and then found himself boxed in on the left by another one. He looked at the mirror, then back ahead. There was just time.

He took his foot completely off the gas and tapped the brake. The car on the left shot ahead, and DeLeon slipped in behind her. He glanced in the side mirror once more, then accelerated across the double yellow line into the oncoming lane. He passed mini-van number two and cut back in ahead of it, then cut again into the right lane and ahead of number one. He braked hard for a moment, just enough to make it over another lane and onto the entrance ramp. To his great satisfaction, the ramp was clear. He was delighted with himself, his anger almost submerged. He cut the wheel just enough to let the rear end step out and went up and around the ramp in a slight drift.

The ramp was the usual three-quarter-circle, like a clock face. You got on at six, went on around past twelve and merged onto the freeway somewhere around two-thirty or three. The Charger reached about eleven on the dial, and if DeLeon had looked out the driver's side window, he'd have been looking north across a triangle of open snow between 275 and its Ford Road exit ramp. If he'd stuck his head out the window and looked down, he'd have seen that the on-ramp was made of concrete with a small edge of asphalt. If he'd looked back, he'd have seen his left rear wheel move off the hard surface onto the softer one. There, where thousands of left wheels had done the same thing, there was a hole. A chunk had been taken out of the side of the ramp, like the side of a cartoon row boat when a shark bites it. DeLeon's left rear wheel dropped down into that hole, moving forward and sideways as well. Another piece of the soft pavement gave way, and the wheel dropped down into eleven inches of hard snow. He panicked and turned hard right, away from the skid; he tried to brake. The physics became complicated.

The Charger spun around its own vertical axis. The front tires were still on pavement and still had traction, but the left rear was in deep snow, trying to move sideways across the surface of the ground. The engineered terrain outside the curve was deliberately flat and featureless, but with a foot or more of accumulated snow and high mounds of it piled up by plowing, there was no longer any guarantee that a car could slide harmlessly to a stop. Instead, the wheel dug in, took the weight of the vehicle and its momentum laterally, and broke its axle. The wheel collapsed, and the Charger twisted violently. It flipped over, landing hard on its top. Hovering overhead, the two *Tisiphone*-class *Erinyes* who were assigned to DeLeon's case exchanged high-fives and flapped quietly away, dragging his soul with them.

Canis aurens The Golden Jackal

Mark Bauer wasn't a knocker. When he wanted you for something, he walked into your office unannounced. If your door was closed, he came in anyway. It was his damn company, after all. This morning, he wanted DeLeon Harper, but Harper's office was dark. So Bauer walked in on the third member of his executive team and asked "You seen Harper?"

Pauleen Prenze was proofreading a recruiting ad and resented the interruption, although she managed not to show it. No, she hadn't seen the CFO. Maybe, she suggested helpfully, he was running late. "Did you ask Carolyn?" Carolyn was the Administrative Assistant they shared.

"She don't know. He ain't called in. Carolyn's tryin' him at home."

"Anything I can help with?" Prenze asked, hoping there wasn't. Most of the company's so-called Directors reported to her, and none of them were worth a damn at personnel issues. When it came to hiring and firing, they were lousy at the former and timid about the latter. The rank and file sales and contract processing people were all under thirty, of assorted genders, and mostly single. Their main area of expertise seemed to be harassing each other and either welcoming it or filing complaints about it. The phone sales area was called "the pit" or "The House of the Rising Sun", depending on how annoyed you might be on a given day. Pauleen was not personally Victorian at all, but she was closer to fifty-five than thirty, and she'd managed to keep most of her clothes on during the bulk of her career. She was also acutely aware that a company like FastFF ought to operate quietly and discreetly; some days, it seemed as though everyone in the place except herself and perhaps Bauer was determined to do the opposite.

"Yeah," Bauer said, closing the door. "We gotta talk about that new thing. The student thing."

"Oh, yes. The student insurance product." She knew what Bauer was talking about: one of the more evil ideas he'd had. "I don't know what Harper came up with, there," she said.

"He said it's legal. Kind of legal. But he don't know if we can do it out-of-state."

"He didn't get that from me." Prenze was a JD although she'd never passed a bar exam. To the extent the company had an in-house counsel, she was it. "I need a while to see where there might be problems."

"That's what I gotta know from him. Will the numbers work if we just do it local? Or do we have to go outside Michigan?" What he meant was that DeLeon owed him a spreadsheet, 128-bit encrypted, demonstrating how many undergraduates they'd have to rob in order to pay for advertising the larceny. The concept was simple enough. You tell high school kids that if they get student loans, they'll graduate from college with tons of debt. And if they don't get jobs or good enough jobs and they can't pay, terrible things will happen. But FastFF will protect you with a Loan Repayment Policy! If you default on your loan, we'll pay off a percentage of it for you! Because we believe you're the future of America!

In fact, the payoff amount would slide with the amount of time you paid into the Policy. If you defaulted on your loan within a few years of graduating (which is when defaults mostly happen), you'd only get back a couple of percent. You'd have to keep paying on both the loans and the policy for twenty years before you'd ever get anything like your money back. And the payout was capped at what you owed, anyway. No matter what happened, you'd never get a check, yourself. The only people FastFF would ever pay would be the folks who did your student loans. And that was Phase One.

In Phase Two, FastFF would bundle the Repayment Policy with – you guessed it! – student loans! We'll loan you your tuition *and* protect you against default! Because we love you! Because we're patriots! Because we're working with an Agency! It says so right in our ads! Look, it has a round, blue logo with gold lettering! And an eagle!

In fact, the so-called agency would be another company, owned by Bauer, that did nothing whatsoever except exist and lend its impressive name (to be determined) and logo to what was basically an intelligence test. Kids and parents foolish enough to buy the idea were dumb. Just dumb. And that, of course, was the Mark Bauer market.

"I'd like to take some more time with this," Pauleen said. "I don't know if we'd qualify as a lender ..."

"Hell, we're a lender now."

"Yes, but the short term loans are separately ..." Somebody knocked on the door. "Yes," she called. Carolyn came in, and she looked shaky.

"Mr. Harper's dead!"

Ailurus fulgens The Red Panda

Andy Patel sighed and rolled over. He fumbled the alarm clock into view; it was just a bit shy of six-thirty. He began sorting out the state of things, mostly by ear, since it was still pitch dark outside, and the blinds were drawn, anyway. He slept deeply, and it usually took him a few seconds to come back to Earth and rejoin humanity.

He closed his eyes and gathered intelligence; he could hear a rushing sound from the bathroom, meaning Jenn was up and showering. A car went by on the street, and it was followed almost at once by an ungodly roar-and-scrape noise. A city snow truck was raising hell on their block, clearing the street and dumping sand as it went. That told him it was winter, still, and there'd probably been some snow overnight. The arm that he reached out told him it was cold, and he drew it back under the covers.

Andy was in many ways the ideal roommate. He'd been involved with just a few women in his life, and none of those relationships had gone as far as moving in. His habits weren't set in stone, and he had no "here's how we used to do it" ideas. He was trainable, something of a blank slate when it came to the daily processes of a dual household, and he took it for granted that Jenn was a representative sample of the human female. When things she did clashed with some assumption of his, he assumed that he'd been wrong and adjusted his point of view.

For example, he'd always thought that singing in the shower was a male thing, but Jenn had altered that notion. Her choice of music was no surprise; he knew she was a folk enthusiast, just as he was. But it still seemed odd to hear a mature and experienced detective and – he smiled just a bit – a modern and enthusiastic lover singing songs with a male perspective and in a harsh lowland Scots accent.

"Mirk and rainy was the necht, there's nae a star in a' the carry" drifted from the shower. She must have moved, because the sound of the water changed and masked the rest of the verse. Then he heard the chorus: "Oh, are ye sleepin' Maggie? Are ye sleepin' Maggie? Ope' the door and let me in, for loud the lynn is roarin' o're the Warlocks craggy."

Jenn's voice was clear and usually sweet, a touch lower than soprano. Closer to mezzo, he thought, and unmistakably a woman's, even when she was voicing lyrics in the manner of Ewan MacColl. It was an untrained voice, and he realized he didn't even know if she could read music. He wasn't used to hearing a woman singing in the shower while he lay in her bed, but he anticipated getting used to it. In a month, they'd have a small, civil wedding. His parents would come, Jenn's daughters, Mac MacArthur and his wife. There'd be a couple of other friends, coworkers of his from the Detroit FBI, colleagues of hers from the Ann Arbor PD. The judge would make some kind of lame "Haven't I seen you in court?" joke for Jenn, and MacArthur would probably reuse his "cooperation among law enforcement agencies" witticism.

The water stopped running, and the resonation changed as Jenn stepped out of the shower. The slight booming from the glass walls vanished, and she sounded a bit higher and sharper. "Blow your worst, ye winds and rain, since Maggie now I'm in aside ye." The song called for "Maggie" to be stretched out into three syllables, and for the 'a' to be given a broad, broad 'ah' pronunciation. Andy was still a bit fuzzy and distractible from sleep, and instead of his future wife singing, he thought of a herdsman in Teviotdale, listening to the lowing of his cattle and hearing "Maggie".

There was a pause, and then she came out into the bedroom. She was wearing a bathrobe; Andy assumed that clothing in the morning was another aspect of woman-ness. In a few months, when the weather warmed up and she'd simply walk into the room nude, he'd be mildly startled.

"Oh, now ye're wakin', Maggie, now ye're wakin', Maggie, what care I for howlett's cry, for boortree banks or Warlocks craggy?" she sang at him. "And what the hell's a boortree bank, anyway?"

"I looked that up once. It's a shrub elder. He's talking about hedge rows, I think." He swung his legs over the edge of the bed, keeping a corner of the sheet over his lap. "And good morning, by the way."

"To you, too," she said, and kissed him on the forehead. "I'll get the coffee going. The shower's all yours."

Andy didn't sing in the shower this morning. His mind kept osculating between the personal and professional, the things he had to deal with that day, things on the job and things on the critical path for getting married. All he really had to do about the latter, Jenn had assured him, was show up. Oh, and invite his parents. "Don't fret," she'd said. "I've done this before." But rings? They'd already had that conversation, and they'd ordered a pair of simple bands. Jenn had declined the offer of an engagement ring, having had one already. It symbolized, she said, the biggest mistake of her life, and she didn't want to do anything as unlucky as that, this time around.

A best man? That was actually harder to work out; Andy'd been in the FBI Detroit office for a couple of years, but he hadn't made firm friends. He had no brothers and only a distant cousin, off on the west coast. "All I've really got is a sister," he said.

"Ask her," Jenn suggested.

"As a best man?"

"Just call her a best person. Come on, it's Ann Arbor. Or would your parents object?" Jenn hadn't met the parents yet.

"No, no. Dad would laugh. And I told you about Mom. She's writing a book on Hinduism, specifically to get it banned in India. On purpose."

"So ask your sister. She's studying something progressive, I think you said."

"I think she'd like it. Probably love it, in fact." He still looked uncertain.

"Issues?" said Jenn.

"You haven't been briefed on that program yet, but I guess you have a need to know, now, being almost family." He was hiding behind security jargon while he picked one of the several ways he'd planned to deal with his sister's reality. "Maria's in a relationship with a woman."

"Shocked, shocked I am," said Jenn, eyebrows theatrically arched. "But then, so are you."

Andy's uncertainty melted. There was a brief mutual display of affection."Sorry," he said. " I didn't think it would be any big issue. But we never talked about it."

"Have I told you the family secret about my daughters? They're a pair of ungrateful, unprincipled Idiots. I hope that isn't a problem for you."

"But you're inviting them, right?"

"The one I have an Email address for, I am." At that moment, Jenn's phone went off. She picked it up and looked at the display. "Oh, dear."

"What?" said Andy.

"It's one of the ungrateful idiots. She must have gotten the invitation."

The Least Weasel Steps Up

Mark Bauer's office was not a masterpiece of interior design, just as the building would never appear in Architectural Digest. It had the tools he needed to run several small, sleazy businesses: a desk and a moderately comfortable chair, a docking station for his laptop, and a charger for his phone. He had two visitor chairs, and some inexpensive, framed dentist-office art because that's what you hung on walls when you were the boss. There was a shredder and a safe, but neither one saw much use. He conducted his business in a digital world, and encryption and disk wiping were quicker and safer than physical destruction. Five to ten percent of his working day could have been described as evidence tampering or obstructing justice.

"Okay," he said. "Temple, you and I ain't talked much since you been here."

Gerald agreed. DeLeon Harper had hired him to do financial reporting and compliance and just introduced him to Bauer. Now Harper was gone and Gerald assumed that Bauer was going to tell him what he'd have to do while they found another CFO. The COO and human resources exec, Ms. Prenze, was in this discussion, too, and that seemed to support his idea.

"But Harper said good things about you. And Pauleen and I think it would be okay for you to take over."

"I'm sorry, Mr. Bauer," said Gerald. "Take over?"

"Yeah, do the CFO job. I need a numbers guy. And somebody who knows the regs." Gerald was stunned.

"I ... ," he started. Pauleen Prenze cut in.

"Mr. Bauer and I feel that it will be easier for you to move into the position. You're used to our environment. If we had to recruit someone ..." She stopped. "If we had to do an outside search, I mean, it would take time. And I think you know that we like to move quickly."

"Yeah," said Bauer. He said "*yeah*" a lot. "We got new ideas. Gotta get goin' on 'em. Hell, we have new ideas all the time."

"And we relied very heavily on Mr. Harper for that," said Pauleen. "He would look at feasibility, profit, legality."

"Legality?" asked Gerald.

"Well, you know," said Bauer. "I mean, not *legality*, so much, but, you know, can we do this? Whatever it is."

"I see."

"'Cause we're always thinking of new stuff. We don't just copycat the industry. We're ..." He searched for the word he wanted. "Innovative. We sort of break new ground a lot."

Gerald remembered a number of unusual questions he'd been asked, things having to do with insurance regulations. All he could think of to say was "I see" again.

"It was very important to us," Pauleen said, "to get a quick yes or no, thumbs up or down on things."

"Yeah, when we have something in the works, we have to move quick. We do it or we don't do it. That's what Harper spent most of his time on."

"And ... the market? Did he look at customers, too?"

"No," said Bauer. "I do that end of it. Basically, if I'm talkin' to you about something, I already know there's customers. I know we can sell it. I just need to know if it'll make money. If we can get away ... if it's ..."

"Compliant," said Pauleen. "If it's valid from a regulatory standpoint."

"Well, thank you," said Gerald. "Thank you. I'll try ... I hope I can do ... what you need. I'll give it my best."

"Okay, good," said Bauer. "Maybe you two can work out the details? Compensation. And security." He looked at Pauleen. "And like that. I gotta make a call."

Gerald left the building a few minutes after six. He was staggering, psychologically, veering from idea to idea. At one moment, he'd feel an adolescent kind of elation, "making" CFO at his age, getting the big promotion, imagining what he'd say when his wife asked "*How was your day?*" The next second, it would be an even more childish terror, an intellectual inadequacy, "*I can't do this!*" And then the adult mentality would react, and he'd cringe from an ethical dope slap. "*Sellout!*" Then the cynic he'd cautiously invited into his personality would sneer and ask "*You think this really happens?*"

And the cynic had things to question. The conversation about "security" had been spooky. He'd had to sign confidentiality agreements that were new to his experience. He'd be getting a company smart phone and leaving his personal device at home. And as he and Pauleen Prenze walked out of the lobby together, she nodded at the "No Firearms" sign. "That doesn't apply to executives, of course," she said. Gerald just nodded, and she let it go at that.

His three-year-old Toyota sedan was at least a familiar hermit's cell. Twice a day, he drove for ninety minutes, and on each trip he could think, sort through the day, and try to arrive at an adjustment of some kind. But as he started home, another threat emerged. If he was going to do this vastly greater job, he might have to become another kind of man. He might have to take the job with him, take calls on the road, bring all that supreme but demanding triviality along with him. And his wife would want to talk, go out, socialize. He'd lose time for thinking, time for weighing up his reactions to the world, time to read.

He almost made a decision then to change his mind, turn the whole thing down. But how to say it? "*I can't take this job because I need time.*" Time for what? Not golf or fishing. Not coaching some pointless youth activity. Not church, not hobbies, not family. How could he say "*My time is worth more than you can pay for*" when he couldn't even put a name on what he did with it? No, he couldn't back out. He'd have to find another way, a plan to steal back the hours. He'd need a third place, not a bar or a cafe, but a place where he could be alone with himself. Jacob would have to find Penuel if he was ever going to see the face of God.

Pardofelis marmorata The Marbled Cat

Jenn walked into the front room, took a deep breath, and answered her phone. "Hi, Jackie."

"Hi, Mom," said her older daughter. "I got your invitation."

"I thought I wouldn't really ask, but I guess I will. What do you think about it?"

"You getting married again? I think ... I think it's fine. If you do, I mean."

"I do," said Jenn. "I've been practicing saying that."

"Good. Good." The girl sounded nervous. "I want to come. For sure. I just ..." Jenn had a horrible premonition that the next phrase would lay out some predicament, an arrest, a pregnancy, a lack of money. She jumped in.

"We'll have a date and a time and all that in a couple of days. Directions and, and, well, directions. I promise I'll send a real paper invitation, too. I'm sorry about the Email, poor manners, and ..."

"Mom."

"What?"

"It's okay. Email is fine."

"Well, good ..."

"But I wanted to ask: is it okay if I bring someone?"

A gallery of Jackie's past boyfriends ran through Jenn's mind. Ignorant, abusive abusers, most of them. How would any of them do in a wedding full of cops?

"Well, of course ..."

"Mom. It's not a boyfriend. " *Oh my God, thought Jenn, she's married one of them.* "I'm just going to say it. I want to bring my partner." A Pause. "Her name is Alice."

Jenn closed her eyes for a full second, clearing her mind. Without knowing it, she'd picked up that habit from MacArthur. Full stop. Delete the table: PreviousAssumptions. Restart.

"Well, of course, Jackie. Of course. I mean, any ..." She almost said "any friend of yours is a friend of mine", but it rang false, considering previous friends, and she made it a lame "Bring anyone you like."

"Mom, I know you think I don't ... I haven't always done, you know, the smart thing."

"*You're a master of understatement, Kid,*" Jenn thought.

"And, you know, um, I'm sorry. But it's different, this is different. I think you'll see it. When you meet Alice. She wants to meet you. And, um, Andy." Jackie paused for breath. "She's right here. Do you want to say Hello?"

"Yes, sure." The phone made a going-to-speaker noise. "We're both here now. Mom, this is Alice."

"Hello, Mrs. Langton," said a surprisingly mature voice. It was pitched in mid-range and with a touch of east coast. "I'm Alice Graves."

"Hello, Alice. And please, just call me Jenn. I haven't even decided if I'm going to stay Langton, or become Patel, or maybe hyphenate ...".

"Yeah, Mom, you could be Langton-Patel," said Jackie.

"Or Patel-Langton," added Alice.

 "Well, it has to fit nicely on a business card," said Jenn. "Oh, Lord, Jackie, did I tell you I'm changing jobs, too?"

The conversation wound down gradually, taking another five minutes to finish. Each of them agreed that she was looking forward to seeing everyone else. Jenn got an address to use for the invitation, and it turned out to be in Ann Arbor. She filed that information; the last she'd known, Jackie was in Chicago. She hung up and found that she was applying another of MacArthur's investigative techniques. "*I just learned something,*" she thought. "*How does it fit? What does it mean?*" It meant, she realized, that her bleak vision of Jackie's future might no longer be operative. She might not become Mrs. Bubba Something with four unhappy children, an address in a mobile home park, and a cameo appearance on some kind of reality TV. Maybe. Maybe she might actually *grow the hell up*.

She walked back out into the small kitchen of her small far-west-side house. Andy was making coffee. In later years, he'd learn how to ignore phone calls until Jenn chose to explain them, but now he couldn't help looking up with a question mark expression.

"Have I told you about when I was abducted by aliens?" Jenn said. "As long as this seems to be laying-cards-on-the-table day?"

The least weasel: Wrestling with an Angel

"So *are* you saying that capitalism should go off and fight fascism while socialism stands by and applauds?" Gerald spoke in a slightly higher voice than his usual tone, and he affected an Oxford accent. "Have you abandoned the idea that socialists can do anything more than choose a side to support?"

He took two paces across the small room. "No, sir, I am saying nothing of the kind." He pitched his voice lower. "I am criticizing those who stand on the left and imagine that there is nothing else in the world to do but favor labor over capital." One of the pieces of furniture was a cheval glass, and he glanced at himself in it. He was wearing a long-tailed coat over a waistcoat and dark trousers. A nylon cravat showed only its knot in the small triangle of space at his throat. "It is not a matter of choosing sides. The side of labor must always be the side of individual freedoms versus the notion of an all-encompassing state. Let alone a religious state."

"I agree." Gerald changed voices again. "But if the only action a socialist will take is to consent to war, or worse, just refrain from opposing it, then he is impotent."

"You and I, Sir, aren't fit to pick up a rifle. Neither are the men and women I'm criticizing."

"But who's to go, then? The young people who will actually go aren't workers, in the sense you mean it. They're the very ones you say capitalism leaves outside the door. They're the unemployed, the disadvantaged, the sons and daughters of poverty. We have no conscription here, Sir! The workers don't fight our wars! And the workers aren't socialists, anyway."

"Calmly. Calmly. The *workers* as you insist on putting it aren't a separate, homogenous class anymore."

"Unfortunately, in your view I suppose."

"Not at all. But it makes it pointless to talk about them as if they were. The main obstacle is that the lowest tiers of society have had their education hijacked by decades of conservative government ..."

"Hijacked? Destroyed is a better word!"

"Use any word you like. The effect is that they've heard nothing of economics. They're not taught that a unified vote can change society. It is not a coincidence, my friend, that competitive athletics and individual celebrities are what capitalism *does* give the disadvantaged class, when it gives them nothing else."

 "I don't follow that, I'm afraid."

"Whether it's intentional or whether it's adaptive, what youth is shown is a vision of success as an *individual* achievement. Whether he has any physical ability or any creative talent is almost irrelevant. He is given pre-packaged dreams in which he is the performer in the center ring, and others exist simply to support him. A dream of community or of making the world safer for everyone is nowhere in the visions his masters ..."

"Oh, seriously! Masters? What masters?"

"You don't think organizations that produce profit from products only bought by the poor are a kind of master? Have you forgotten company towns, company stores? They were able to force workers to buy one thing and not another. Today, the difference is that the masters must persuade and condition."

"All right, all right. But we've strayed from the point. I say that no war is supportable, and you seem to be disagreeing with me. Unless I've completely misunderstood you."

"No, I'm afraid you haven't. And I do disagree with you – unless I've misunderstood *you* –when you seem to say that any collection of people has a right to self-determination, regardless of what it is they're trying to determine."

"I never said that."

"You imply it. You oppose war, even against what are clearly fascist movements. Even if the fighters are gravely deluded and savagely lied to by their leaders. Now if you question the *conduct* of such wars, the capability and intelligence of our military and our governments, that's another matter entirely. I question it myself." Outside, a siren kicked off, and the emergency vehicle, whatever it was, charged by the apartment.

"*Damn*," thought Gerald. He went to the window and pulled aside the drapes. The bleak suburban street was still in motion, but the excitement had moved on. A truck downshifted and snarled by. "*Sidetracked again. We were almost there, and then he started with the war topic again.*" He tried to reengage with his counterpart.

"But if a man does some work, and it is arguably exploitive, still he pays taxes. And those taxes support the poor, surely? "

He turned toward the imitation fireplace, and sighed. He clasped his hands behind his back.

"This is nothing new, you realize? You bring this up every time, and every time, I remind you that support is not the thing you imagine it to be."

"And every time, I remind you that whatever you call it, taxes feed people."

"How can you not understand? You're talking about the dole. Giving people enough money to continue to live at the bottom of the ladder is not support. Support like that turns malignant after the first generation. A man who has supported himself and loses his job still remembers freedom and can realistically hope to recover it. A child born on the dole never knows anything else. You're talking about support as if it's some general kind of goodwill, and I'm talking about support as defense against needing support in the first place."

"We keep coming back to this, I see."

"Yes, we do. Because you want capitalism to be free to do what it wants to and take care of its victims along the way. I want it to be kept from having victims. Frankly, that's the crux of our disagreement."

Gerald turned and without meaning to, he saw himself in the long mirror again. His expression disappeared; he'd been mildly exalted, beginning to be swept along in the power of his own rhetoric, but at the sight of himself, it dropped off like a mask. His shoulders dropped, too, a bit, and he stepped away. He sat down in a cushioned yard-sale chair, made of cheap white wood and stained clumsily to look like something else. He took off his glasses, cradled his head in his hands, and massaged his eyes and forehead. "*Shit*," he thought, and winced slightly, like a man who'd been brought up not to swear. Guilt appeared at once. Gerald had never performed any kind of non-standard sex act, never looked at Internet pornography, never abused a drug or an animal. But these nights with his selves were as deeply shameful and disappointing to him as the worst kind of vice.   He stood up and walked into the empty bedroom. He changed his clothes, hanging the Victorian costume in the bare closet. His twenty-first century watch told him that in ten and half hours, he'd be back in the office. "*Shit*," he thought again.

Mustela nudipas The Barefoot Weasel

Downtown Ann Arbor in the small hours of a winter morning is a different animal.   Until the bars close, there are still people on the sidewalks, but they move quickly from one place to another, from cars to clubs and back again. There are few groups hanging out, a few people pushing the limits of smoking bans. The homeless are almost invisible, gone to the shelters, to the one or two camps below bridges, gone south. Students walk fast   toward campus housing or off into the efficiency neighborhoods. Out of town patrons drive away, back to the suburbs. If there's trouble, it will have already happened or it will happen soon, before everything empties out and everyone goes home to bed. By three o'clock, things will be very quiet.

Jeri Klein liked to drive these cold, dark shifts. The radio traffic would taper off, spiking once in a while to deal with a domestic call or an accident. Then it would go quiet again, and she'd carry on with her stalking. Wherever she was, she'd drop down to the patrol car's minimum speed, foot off the gas and just idling along. Her eyes would move like a pilot's: left, ahead, mirror, right, instruments, ahead.   She was attuned to movement, catching things with her peripheral vision, and if she was gliding down a residential street, she'd turn the headlights off and slip quietly along in the shadows between the street lights. The tires made a crunching sound on the snow or a faint hiss on dry pavement.

On those nights, when she was just out there *watching*, it seemed like a higher form of duty than other police work. She was the night watch, looking for trouble in the literal sense. She ghosted past dark houses, glancing down alleys and side streets. She noted the windows that were still lighted and the porch lights that were turned off. When a call took her somewhere close, she'd drive by the house of a friend or her mother's house; why not? They paid taxes.

Tonight, she'd been out on the west side, checking an alarm on a tire store. Nothing. By the time she got there, the alarm was silent, the doors locked. Not uncommon in extreme weather, or maybe someone yanked on a door and then thought better of it. She walked around the building and saw nothing at all. She started her car again, and the dashboard said that it was ten below zero outside. Coming back into town, she gave her status as "Patrol", and turned south on Seventh. It was all residential here, dark and quiet. She dropped her speed to a crawl and went up the slight hill toward Madison. She turned there and went east; at least near Main Street there were businesses.

She went gently on down the other side of the hill, blacked out, and enjoying the invisibility. There was no one to see her, anyway, but still it was exhilarating. As she approached Main, a vehicle came from the right and turned without signaling onto Madison, heading away from her. It went halfway down the block, and the brake lights came on. It turned into the lumber yard.

Jeri lit up her headlights and accelerated. The target was out of sight, but she knew that the space it turned into went between two lines of lumber sheds, across a paved lot that was narrowed by railroad tracks and then out onto Hill street. It could get away. She bounced over the near end of those same tracks and turned in after the vehicle. She still hadn't called in because she didn't know if there was anything wrong. It seemed, though, that the number of legitimate reasons for a car being down there at four in the morning were few.

Ahead of her, she saw the vehicle – a pickup truck, actually – stopped in a space cleared of snow. The driver's door was opening. Twenty feet back, she stopped and hit her blue lights, mostly as identification. The driver got out and stood staring at her. She opened her own door and trained her spot light on him: an older man in a parka and knit cap. "Stay in the truck," she ordered.

Half an hour later, she was back at the Department. "So, you know, that manager down at Fingerle's wasn't all that happy," the Sergeant said. "Didn't like being yelled at in his own lumber yard."

"I got that impression," Jeri admitted. She was finishing up the details of her shift, and explaining the forceful stance she'd taken while investigating a suspicious vehicle. She'd initially called it a possible break in, but the Sergeant overruled that term. "Let's not get too dramatic," he'd said.

The Swift Fox and the Red Panda

As usual, Frank and Miriam Patel were early. This was because Frank had a bad case of Jesuit-induced obsessiveness, something he'd been deliberately trying to get over for decades. He'd experienced a brief period of Lamarckian angst, fearing that his own education had somehow influenced his son's psychology, even though the father had run screaming from the Church at an early age. He'd never done anything but discourage religion and rigorousness in the boy. And yet the offspring had gone off and joined the Marines. And then the FBI. Miriam laughed at this idea, pointing out that if Andy wanted order and discipline, it was because neither of his parents had any to offer. Both were tenured academics at Case Western, and neither one gave a fig for propriety. Miriam had brought the Patel name to the partnership, and in typical contrary fashion, they'd decided to go with that. Actually, they made a bet on whose thesis would be approved first, and the winner got to keep his or her name.

Now, they were standing awkwardly in a Judge's office in Ann Arbor, waiting for the remainder of the wedding party. The Judge stuck his head in periodically, checking on status. Eventually Jenn and Andy showed up, along with Andy's sister and Best Person, Maria. There was a brief delay, and then Mac and Colleen arrived; Colleen was playing Best Person for the Bride's side. They were immediately followed by Jenn's daughter and her partner. The Judge, long accustomed to non-traditional assortments among wedding participants, didn't blink an eye. For him, the Cop-marries-Fed aspect of it was more notable and much funnier.

Jenn wore one of the suits she'd acquired for her new job. She'd tried to get Andy to wear his Marine uniform, but instead he wore his FBI dress blacks – that is, a dark suit, white shirt, and black tie. When he'd finished dressing that morning, he'd walked out of the bedroom "wearing a wire" -- a large stage microphone sticking out of his breast pocket. Jenn convinced him that it clashed with his shoes. Already he was discovering the value of humor in a relationship.

The Judge stood behind his desk and in front of bookcases filled with law books – or else a very skillfully painted *trompe l'oeil* rendition of them. Everyone else stood as well, since there wasn't room for a lot of chairs, and nobody wanted to encourage long-winded weddings, anyway. *If you want that kind of wedding, get a church*, was the general policy. It was 8:30 in the morning, and only Mac and Colleen had managed to get any coffee.

For Andy, the stress of this event had been all in the run up to it. He had no doubts whatsoever, and now that he was here and nothing had gone wrong, he felt suddenly relaxed. The decisions were all made, the details all handled. All the necessary people were in the room. Things could now go on automatically. He read off his lines from the vows script, and then found himself looking at Jenn and watching her as she read hers. They'd written them together, carefully leaving out any notion that either party would "obey" the other. His attention narrowed to Jenn and the lines of her face. She'd stopped speaking, and he distantly noted that the Judge was saying something. Andy just kept looking at Jenn.

One of the guests chuckled softly, and Jenn smiled . She recognized this lapse of attention; he was having an "Andy moment" as she called it. Before he could recover on his own, she turned toward him with her hands on her hips and said in her command voice, "Sir, you have the right not to remain silent. Anything you don't say will be held against you."

Andy quickly reestablished his grip on reality, snapped to attention, and said "Ma'm, yes, Ma'm! I do!"

The audience cracked up. The judge forgot his painful arches, stepped back, and nearly tripped over his desk chair. What minimal ice there had been was broken. His Honor made a partial attempt to compete by proclaiming them Fed and Cop, and telling Andy he could kiss the Officer. That fell pretty flat, but the room gave him a polite laugh anyway, and no one noticed that Alice and Jackie let go of each others' hands self-consciously. Even Mac missed it.

There was a lunch gathering later on, meeting a few more people at a newly-opened bistro on Liberty. No one bothered with place cards or seating, and more or less as a result of random shuffling, Mac sat down between Colleen and Alice

Graves. It wasn't the quietest room, with everyone there trying to talk, plates banging around in the kitchen, and some kind of recorded noise being played. Mac assumed it was music, but he was damned if he knew what. Throughout the restaurant, as more customers were seated, each person tried to make himself heard by ratcheting up the volume of his voice, and every increase in the ambient level constricted the bubble within which Mac could hear. Just across the table, Miriam Patel tried to say something to him, and he smiled and nodded. "*I hope it wasn't anything profound.*" he thought. He could hear Colleen talking to a colleague of Andy's, and he realized that the only other person in earshot would be Alice.

"I don't think I quite understood what you do," he said. It was slightly misleading, because no one had told him much about her at all.

"I'm just starting on my post-doctoral work," she said. Mac was pleased to see that she spoke very clearly and loud enough that he could hear most of it.

"Here at the U?"

"Yes. I'm in Anthropology. And Jackie said you worked with her mother?"

"For years, yes."

"She said you were her teacher ... or mentor? Is that right?"

"Well, I probably showed her a lot of ways *not* to do things. She probably taught me more than vice versa. On balance." Mac felt oddly unwilling to talk about it. For one thing, the main reason he'd been asked to work with Jenn was that she'd annoyed the FBI, early on, and he'd had to mend fences for her. After this marriage had lasted, say, ten successful years, he might feel comfortable making a joke about that old problem.

Not now. And another thing: their time of working together was over. If she ran into problems with her new gig, there wasn't going to be much he could do to help. "*Christ*," he thought, "*I'm getting maudlin in my old age.*"

Alice looked slightly unsatisfied with that answer, but Mac steered the talk back toward her affairs.

"Am I right that Jackie is in school here, too?" He knew it was. Jenn was extremely happy about it.

"Yes, yes she is." Alice managed to sound both pleased and uncertain. "She's accepted for the fall. At Eastern Michigan. They have an International business program."

"Ah, interesting."

"Her idea is to try for the International Relations program here."

"*When will I stop interrogating people?*" Mac thought. All of his experience with the things people say wouldn't let him parse the feelings underlying her last statement. It sounded flat and somewhat disguised. If Alice had an opinion of Jackie's ambitions, she wasn't prepared to imply a thing about them. And if she'd said "*As if!*", it was none of his business, anyway.

"You know," she said, " Jackie's mother suggested that I ... that I talk to you about a situation."

"Really?" said Mac. He was instantly alert, wary, a bit on guard. Usually an opening like that led to a discussion of traffic tickets or a really good boy who just made a mistake and ... But once in a while, there was something interesting going on.

"Yes. I have a cousin, and he's not, well, responding. I mean, he's missing, I'm afraid I have to say."

"You're afraid to say?"

"Um, yes, I guess I have to call it that. We talk all the time, almost every day. But it's been a week now. And he'd call or text or something, I'm sure."

"And he's not just busy or out of town or ...", Mac left the question hanging.

"Well, his wife says she doesn't know, either." That made it more interesting. Mac turned in his chair, partly to hear her more clearly, partly to ease a growing ache in his hips.

"Is that all she says?"

"We don't have a lot to say to each other," Alice said. "She's never been very forthcoming with me."

"Hmmm," said Mac. "And you've tried calling him at work?"

"They just say he's not in the office. And I finally called the Police ..."

"Which Police?" Mac asked. It made a great deal of difference.

"I called the number for the city he lives in. Grosse Pointe ... Place, I think."

"Grosse Point Park, maybe?"

"Yes, that's right. It's a suburb. But he worked here in Ann Arbor. He *works* here, I mean."

"Ah," said Mac. He noted the change from past to present tense. "And did you talk to anyone here, too?"

"No, no, I didn't. I thought ... he's missing from where he lives. But he spent a lot of time here, too. Should I have called the Police here?"

"Not necessarily. I assume the people in Grosse Pointe explained that adults are allowed to be missing for quite a while? That there has to be something more than that before cops get involved? Ann Arbor would have told you the same thing."

"Yes, that's what they said. But I know he'd have called me."

Both Mac and Alice kept checking for other conversations or questions, but in general, people were leaving them alone. No one but Jackie knew Alice, and Jackie was down at the other end of the table, talking to her mother in a way that was very new for both of them. Everyone who knew Mac knew that he couldn't hear worth a damn in settings like this, and they were content to catch up with him later, in quieter surroundings. So he and Alice kept talking, and Mac learned that she and her cousin were largely isolated from their families, both out of touch with parents and both in relationships that didn't play well with the relatives.

"They don't like the choices I've made," she said, "And his wife is difficult. She made him move out here, for example, because it's where she grew up."

"In the suburbs?"

"Yes, one of the Grosse Pointes."

"But you were close? And he talked to you frequently?"

"He did. About literature, mostly. And politics. And, oh, social things. He was always aware of injustices and unfairnesses. He was ... it sounds odd, a finance executive, you know, but I got the sense that he was thinking almost like a socialist." She smiled. "It sounds a little like a dirty word today, doesn't it?"

"Well, it's something to call your opponents, anyway," said Mac. He took a sip of his wine. "You can count on most people not knowing what it means."

"Oh, I agree!" she said. "He hated that. People calling the President a fascist and a socialist in the same sentence. "

"Dammit", thought Mac. *"Politics. Next, we'll be talking about religion."* He grasped for a transition. "You got the impression he was unhappy?"

"Unhappy ... yes. He felt bad about inequality, mostly. He kept coming back to that. And responsibility."

"Did he seem depressed?"

"Well, I don't ... oh, yes, I see. You mean enough to hurt himself?"

"That's one of the ways people disappear." Mac regretted that sentence immediately. Alice looked away. When she turned back, her eyes were harder.

"No," she said. "He wouldn't do that. It wasn't something he could do. It would have been irresponsible." Her voice softened slightly, but her eyes kept a look of certainty. "But he might have ..."

A pause. "He might have ...?"

"He might have gone off to do something, somewhere. Somewhere where he could be hurt. That, I think he could do."

"Did he ever talk about that?"

"No. Not directly. But, you know, between here and the suburbs, there are so many ... there's so much need. So many places where you could go in all innocence, go to try to help, and end up getting hurt."

Mac said nothing. He faulted himself for not noticing two cocktail glasses in front of her, empty, with their plastic stir sticks laying on the table.

"I hate saying that," Alice said. "It sounds ... racist or prejudiced or ... insensitive. I've never been anywhere like that, myself. I don't know about it. I've never helped build a house or hand out food or ... I have no right ..." She turned away again and put her napkin up to her face.

MacArthur reached for his wine glass again, noticed that it was also empty. "*Dammit, dammit,*" he thought.

Alice turned back to him, forcing a smile. "I always cry at weddings," she said.

"Yeah, " said Mac. "Let me see what I can come up with." He found his pen and pulled over a napkin. "First things first. What's your cousin's name?"

"Gerald," she said. "Fisher Gerald Temple."

Mustela sp. The Undescribed Weasel

"Affordable housing," said Mac.

Colleen looked up from her tablet. "What about it?"

"I try to keep up with political euphemisms," he said. "But that one seems to have crowded out everything else. I missed that."

"Missed what?"

79

"I missed the point where we stopped saying "low-income" housing. I understand why "housing project" went away. Bad memories there. But now "affordable" is what everybody thinks we need. But not in our backyards, according to this."

"Whose backyards?" Colleen asked, trying to keep her place in an article about Medicare fraud.

"Up on the north side, I guess. Here's a developer, some guy from Bloomfield Hills. He wants to build "mixed-use" stuff, and he's specifically saying that affordable housing *isn't* planned. So the opposite of "affordable" is ...?"

"Unaffordable."

"Apparently. I guess he plans on it standing empty."

"I've known developers like that. " Colleen went back to her tale of remarkably ill-concealed malfeasance on the part of a pharmacy owner. "Did you see this bit about the guy in Livonia? Independent pharmacy. He got his son to hack the point-of-purchase systems and just multiply everything by two."

"By two?"

"Yep. Receipts said two bottles of pills, two packages of insulin, everything. Customers never checked, since they only paid one co-pay. And if anybody did ask, the clerks would just call it a typo and fix it."

"Idiots," said Mac, absently. He was already off to another site, reading about one of the many parts of the world where people were butchering each other. Dinner at the MacArthur's was like a news show with long gaps in the commentary.

Four miles or so west of Mac's dinner table, two young men were standing in a doorway. It was a dark recess. They could be seen only from the parking lot in front of them, and then only from a narrow angle. The doorway was not theirs. It belonged to a vacant unit in a large development, built in the Sixties as a "Low Income Housing Project." In those days, it was considered laudable to fund this kind of thing; coincidentally, of course, most of them were out on the edges of town. In the forty-odd years since the apartments and townhouses were built, they'd gone through good times and bad. In the nineties, the development had been as close to a dangerous neighborhood as Ann Arbor really had. The real estate boom in the next decade didn't help, since it took lots of people out of the rental market. There were signs of recovery now, but there were still empty units and a disproportionate number of technically unemployed young people. The two teens in the doorway were among them.

There was a small amount of snow falling, and the wind was bitter. They were dressed against the cold, wearing hooded sweatshirts with jackets over them. One had a stocking cap pulled over his ears, and the other had his hood up. They were there because they were sales representatives, the housing complex was their territory, and this doorway was their office. If someone drove up and stopped and if the person and the car looked unthreatening (that is, if it wasn't obviously a police vehicle), they would move quickly to the near-side window and sell the occupant a retail amount of heroin. Heroin was the fad drug at the moment, cheaper and hipper than cocaine, and not so quickly toxic as methamphetamines. Heroin killed its users, but not as publically as other substances.

A car came into the lot, but it turned immediately into a parking space half way down the drive. The boys watched with interest but not a great deal of it. A customer or a cop would have come directly to them. Mostly out of boredom, they watched a woman get out, unload a child from the back seat, and enter a unit. It was half past nine. A minute later, another set of headlights appeared, turning in and heading slowly down toward them. They drew back further into the shadow and watched. It came on at low speed and without hesitating. "Jeep" said one of them to the other, and they relaxed. No matter how practical it might have been, the Ann Arbor police didn't drive Jeeps. They had an SUV, but it was bigger, and it had light bars. The car slowed even more and then stopped, almost in front of their door.

They walked slowly toward it, sticking to the shoveled, icy walk; the snow was piled up two feet deep on each side. The driver's window came down. The person driving was a black woman, somewhere above thirty, wearing dark clothes and a balaclava, otherwise known as a ski mask.

The older of the boys, called Deano, leaned on the car, glancing around the inside for threats, just as a policeman would have done. The driver was alone. "What you need?" he asked.

The driver slammed the door open, knocking him backward and onto his colleague. Both lost their footing and fell. The woman jumped out, holding an automatic pistol. The two boys were scrambling frantically, each trying to use the other as support. The younger one succeeded in getting out from under his friend, accidentally kicking him in the head in the process. Deano had been knocked on his back, and now he managed to roll over ; he started to do a push-up movement in order to get on his feet, but the woman planted her foot in the middle of his back and shoved him down on his face. He felt pressure behind his right knee. The woman shoved the muzzle of her gun hard against him and fired one shot, destroying the lower end of his femur and shattering his knee cap. The other boy jumped over the snow mound, fell, got back up, and floundered off. The woman tossed her weapon over the other pile of snow, got back in her car, and drove away.

Lights began to come on in the apartments. Although there were two couples and one father-son pair who were prone to shouting at each other and sometimes throwing a punch or two, gunshots weren't commonplace. Not at all. Nor was someone lying on the sidewalk, screaming in pain. It didn't take long for Deano to become the center of attention, surrounded by Police officers and EMT people. In a little more time, he was on a stretcher and headed off to the University Hospital's Emergency room. It took much longer to finish with the investigation; the other boy was nowhere around, his tracks ending on a shoveled walk. There was the gun, of course, and the small amount of a controlled substance that Deano hadn't been able to dispose of. But Deano wasn't saying anything useful, and although most people in the area had heard the shot, no one had been looking out. "Nobody saw nothin'," as a patrol officer said to his sergeant.

"I guess he pissed somebody off," the sergeant said.

"I guess so."

The Least Weasel Beyond Penuel

"So lemme tell you about this idea," said Mark Bauer. Gerald sat rigidly across from him, keeping his face blank. Only his breathing indicated anything. It was short and controlled, like that of a man waiting to hear a diagnosis or a verdict. He had a legal pad; Bauer glanced at it. "No notes, by the way. Confidential." Gerald nodded.

"Yeah, so. I keep seeing these commercials for car insurance. They push how it's fast and easy and even anonymous, for Christ's sake. And you get your proof of insurance instantly. And it's cheap, supposedly." He looked at Gerald. "What does that tell you about who they're selling to?"

Gerald had seen the ads. Cartoon characters, happy-looking young people. No senior citizens. "Well, young people, I guess. People starting out in life." Bauer wasn't nodding. "Maybe ... ah, single people. Without children?" He couldn't recall any kids in the ads.

"Yeah. Partly. But who wakes up in a panic and needs car insurance fast? And instant proof of insurance?"

"Somebody who ... who just got a ticket? For not having it?"

"Yup. That's the idea. Somebody who's been sleazing along for a while without it. Or they had it and didn't pay the bills. And now they gotta renew the license. Or, like you say, they got a ticket and they have to show up with proof, or it'll cost 'em."

"I see," said Gerald.

"And when they check with one of these sites, they get a bunch of options, and some of 'em are really cheap. But they don't cover shit. If they want real insurance, it costs more. More than a big insurance company, maybe. And then, they say "driving record no problem". Yeah, it's no problem, they'll cover you. But it costs like hell if you got tickets and accidents. But you're there, you got problems, you don't wanna shop around. You just want it over with. So you click and screw yourself."

"But you say there are already a number of these companies working? Is there room for us to, um, enter the market?"

"No. Not just to copy 'em. And we don't wanna do that, anyway. But I look at this, and what do I see underneath it all?"

"I'm not sure," said Gerald. He genuinely didn't want to know.

"I see what the real product is. Think about some kid, he's outta high school, one way or the other. Maybe he's got a bullshit job or maybe he doesn't. But he lives where there's no bus to take, he's gotta drive or he's gonna look lame. Girls don't like bus riders. He's got some piece of shit car, maybe he bought it from his uncle or something. Or grandma gave it to him. But it ain't insured. Maybe it ain't even registered. But he's driving it. What is he?"

"Disadvantaged?"

"No, he's angry. Why? Because he's like that comic, what's his name, he don't get no respect?"

"Rodney Dangerfield."

"Yeah. This kid thinks he's disrespected. He don't think he's dumb, he ain't ashamed of himself. He's pissed off because he has to panic every time he sees a cop car. And every time he buys gas, he has to pay cash, go inside and hand it over before he pumps. He ain't got no credit card. And even worse than that?

"What?"

"He ain't got no driver's license, either."

"Okay, uh, Mr. Bauer. I think I see ... but isn't this fellow also, ah, broke? If we're thinking about him as a customer, I don't see ..."

"Yeah, even I'm not stupid enough to try to sell to somebody who's got *no* money. But aren't we in some other lines of business, kind of similar to this? For example, why don't this guy have a credit card?"

"Well, I assume because he's got no credit."

"Right. And what do we do for people like that?"

"Oh." Gerald felt a cold streak in his vertebrae. "The debit card product line."

"Right. And what do we know for sure about those people? We know for sure how much money they have. And you know why somebody without much money and no credit buys into our debit card thing? Respect. They can carry cash around and always feel like a chump, or they can whip out our card and feel like somebody. And half of 'em don't even know the difference between credit and debit until they overdraw it once or twice."

"So how ... how would you see this ... working?"

"We do a new website. We do commercials like "Get the respect you deserve". "Solve your driving problems with one click!" Driving problems is like a code for "no insurance." And when they click, they get a choice. Real insurance, which we'll sell off to some other company. There's plenty of carriers out there that'll write policies. And we'll make that cheap. Because

86

the other option is big margin. Because why? Because it ain't really insurance."

"Not insurance?" Gerald was beginning to feel sick.

"Nope. We invent some kind of name for it, maybe like "affordable guarantee policy" or coverage spelled with a K or something. We'll work on that. And in the fine print, it's just like an extended warranty on your own car. It covers "massive emergency issues" or something. All mechanical, all repair, no totaling anything, no replacement costs, and sure as hell, no goddamn liability. But you gotta read the fine print like a lawyer to find that out. And plus, we throw in a free photo ID. You send us a picture, give us some other info, and we give you a pretty card that maybe somebody blind and stupid would think might be something official."

"But the state won't accept that! Nobody will!"

"Right. They won't. But our boy won't know that. We'll write it up so we never promise it'll be good with the Secretary of State or the Cops or anybody else. If he buys the legit policy, he'll be okay, but if not, hey, you're idiot enough to buy something like this, you gonna read the agreement? And here's the other thing. If he's got a printer, he can print out a "Certificate of Indemnity" or something like that. And he'll think it's a proof of insurance. And it'll look something like it, but it won't actually try to be a fake. And he'll whip it out when he gets pulled over, and well ... sorry."

"But how long could we keep this up? What happens when the first of our ... our customers gets stopped. Or in an accident. Or even goes to get his car registered?"

"That's where Pauleen comes in. The kid says "I got these papers." The cops say "They're bogus." They send somebody to talk to us. And Pauleen shows 'em the terms and conditions.

Shows 'em the records of the kid clicking on "I accept". Shows 'em the fine print that says "I know this ain't a real ... gobbledygook, whatever the legal term is for whatever our thing isn't. And in maybe ten years, the guys in Lansing get around to passing a law against what we're doing. And then we stop. In fact, we've probably stopped already, you know, because we thought of something better by then."

Bauer paused for a sip of cold coffee. "And you know, speaking of Pauleen, that gives me another idea." Gerald almost gasped. "People look at somebody with letters on their name – letters behind their name, I mean. Hers says JD, and people watch themselves when they see that. You got that MSF thing going. That's impressive. But it's a lot of work, right? Lots of money. Lots of time. Maybe we could hook up with some of those for-profit colleges, give people some letters." Gerald's stomach heaved. He started to sweat.

"Or ... here's maybe an even better idea. We don't hook up with anybody. We just dream up some titles, give some kind of bogus test, hand out certificates. Presto."

"Mr. Bauer," Gerald said, "Excuse me for just a minute. I just have to ... go to the restroom." He got up and walked quickly down the hall. "Jeez," Bauer thought. "He must be sick."

Gerald was gone five minutes. When he came back, he was pale, but he seemed to be in control. "You all right?" asked Bauer.

"Yes, Mr. Bauer, I ..."

"Yeah, you know, drop the Mister thing. I call you Temple, you call me Bauer. We're a kind of last name company here. Should have said that before, I guess."

"Oh, well, thank you. I'll do that. Look, I ..."

"While you were out, I thought of something else. What's more disrespectful than getting pulled over? What do you want to do most of all when a Cop's leaning on your car? You want to throw a little scare into him, too, make him think he's dealing with somebody, not just some kid." Gerald stared at him.

"So we give him some kind of business card, "Citizen's Legal Advisors" or something. "We sue!" Something that says "*I'm a big shot. I got an attorney. Fuck with the bull and you get the horn.*" Get it?"

"Yes, I see it," said Gerald. "Cut rate insurance. Meaningless ID. A pretend big shot. Yes, I see it. But I think we're missing something here."

"What's that?"

"We could offer ordination." Bauer looked blank. "We could come up with a religion, and make people priests. Or nuns. Why, for the top of the line, why not sainthood? Now, that's respect."

Bauer's face was blank. He looked at Gerald for a few seconds, and then he said "No. I thought of that priest thing already. Already been done. You can be a minister on the net for five dollars. Good idea, though."

Gerald was stunned into silence. He listened to Bauer's last few ideas, and pretended to be noting the research that would be necessary. He managed to leave the room without falling. He took a few steps toward his own office, but after a pause, he went on a few more to Pauleen's door. He stuck his head in. "I've just had a conversation with Mr. Bauer. About his new ideas."

"Yes?"

"Do you think he was kidding?"

Pauleen said no, Mr. Bauer was always very serious about business matters. Gerald managed to nod. His head was pounding, and his mouth was dry. Later, after Gerald left the building, Bauer dropped in on Pauleen.

"I was talkin' to Temple. He thinks we ought to make people priests and saints and nuns."

"Really?"

"Yeah, really. You think he was kidding?"

Funambulus pennantii The Northern Palm Squirrel

"Ooooh. Shit." A student leaned back from her desk and stretched, arching her back and clasping her hands behind her neck. The paper she was writing was eighty percent done. She twisted her neck back and forth; the clock display at the bottom of the screen said 2:57 AM, and she was desperately bored. "Five minutes break," she thought and stood up. Stretching again, she looked out the window.

Observatory was snow-covered, and the lights didn't counteract your initial sense of darkness; it was a dark street. On her side, it was lined with university buildings, but on the east you saw just the blackness of the Forest Hills cemetery. Cars were parked everywhere it was permitted, but nothing moved. She turned back to her desk, walked to the end of the tiny room and back, and looked out again.

This time there was movement. A person, a woman, was walking along the far side. She was wrapped in a parka with the hood up. Snow that had been pushed off the sidewalk made a barrier with the street, and on the other side, a formal iron fence ran along the edge of the cemetery. Suddenly, the woman on the street reacted as though she'd heard something. She pivoted to her right, toward the fence. As she did, a man took one more long running stride out of the woods, put his hands on the top fence bar, and vaulted over onto the sidewalk.

The woman neither ran nor seemed to be screaming. She shifted her posture, turning her head to face the man, but keeping her body side-on to him. He slipped, caught his balance, and charged at her. Something happened then that was too fast to understand, so fast that it seemed almost not to happen at all. The man moved past on the fence side (or did the woman step aside?), she made a small, almost gentle-looking movement with her right arm against his back, and somehow instead of running he was flying. He struck the frozen ground with his head and slid at least a meter on his face. He may or may not have started to get up, but the woman twisted again, and her booted right foot slammed across the back of his skull. She spun all the way around, and as she completed the turn, planted her toe between his legs. This kick was hard enough to move him a few inches forward. It seemed that she may have slipped herself, or maybe she dropped to one knee deliberately. Kneeling beside the man, she twisted his left arm backward and up. She leaned on it slightly, and this time the scream was audible through the student's closed window. The woman got up, took two steps past the man, and kicked him hard in the face. Then she ran, not slipping at all, down the street and out of sight. The student fumbled for her phone.

Detective Louie Burke showed up in reasonably good time. The University Hospital emergency room was barely four blocks away, but he and the ambulance got there together. There were also two patrol cars from the University police, but this was a boundary street, University on one side, the cemetery on

91

the other, and there was an agreement to cooperate on serious crimes, anyway.

"We got a fight call from a girl in Stockwell," said a Campus Cop. He pointed at the dormitory. "We found this guy lying here all busted up and no assailant."

"So, what's it look like? Two drunks? Any descriptions?" Burke was used to assault calls about this time of night.

"Nothing yet. We're a little busy getting him packaged up." He nodded at the ambulance crew getting the man up off the ice and onto a gurney. This was not really taking up any of the officer's time, but he actively disliked Burke, having dealt with him before, and if anyone was going to stumble around in a dorm, waking up kiddies and getting useless information from them, it might as well be this loud and somewhat arrogant little City Cop. The two local agencies of armed state coercion weren't the best of friends.

Burke missed these subtleties. He wasn't at all arrogant, actually, just oblivious. He had no idea how he appeared to other people, and he was stressed and unhappy because his work load had doubled with Jenn Langton's departure. "Fuck," he said. "All I need, another assault thing to figure out. You said the other half of it booked?"

"No, I said we didn't see him or her leave. Or they. Unless he did all that to himself."

"Okay," said Burke. He walked over to the EMT people. "Where's he going?"

The ambulance driver looked at him in mild disbelief. "Oh, I guess we'll take him to Detroit Receiving."

"Really?" Burke could see several University hospital buildings from where he was standing. The ER was just across the health system campus. "I thought you'd take him over there."

"Well, if you insist, yes, we'll take him down the road here. See if they've got anybody who can fix a dislocated shoulder."

Burke had a vague feeling he was being yanked around, but it didn't take hold. He just went right on with his work. "So, a dislocated shoulder? Anything else?"

"Oh, yeah. Looks like a broken eye socket, a blow and some cuts on the back of the head. Nose is mashed pretty good. The way he was holding himself, probably got kicked in the nuts, too."

"Jeez," said Burke.

"Hey, Burke!" said the other UM officer, touching him on the back. "We got a witness here." He was standing beside the student. "Says she saw it all, out her window."

It took a couple of passes through the story before Burke felt confident he had it down. Woman walks down street. Man jumps fence, attacks her. She stomps him into the snow. Maybe some martial arts, no weapons evident. Woman runs – literally runs – away down slippery sidewalk. Vanishes.

"Okay," said Burke. "I think I got it. Oh, what did the woman look like?"

The student thought about it. "She was all bundled up. And she was tall."

"How about race, you know, African-American, white ..."

"I don't know," she said. "She was wearing a ski mask."

Hylobates lar The Lar Gibbon

A man stood on a sloping beach, looking west into the blank gray ice fog. Ahead, the surface of a frozen loch stretched out of sight, blank white under clouds. Overnight, the snow had blown clear, then the wind dropped and a freezing fog had rolled in. His beard and long hair were stiffening with tiny drops of ice, and it cracked off his clothes as he moved. Behind him a black stone, a meter high, was coated and glistening.

On a clearer day, he'd stand by the rock and take a sighting from a tall tree on the west shore. He'd walk a hundred and twenty paces toward it in a straight line and come to his hole in the ice. Today, he couldn't see more than fifteen paces in any direction, but he needed to go. He was low on food, and the lake teemed with fish. It wasn't really a dangerous walk, just unpleasant, stumbling around, looking for his personal spear hole.

He set off, carrying a sheepskin bag , a line made of twisted wool, and his fish spear. The point was carefully made from a pair of long bones, mounted at an angle to each other and serrated on the inside edges. It looked like a pair of spread fingers, and it was darkened with use, stained with fish blood. Everything he wore, head to toe, was sheepskin, with or without the wool left on. The only color was on his conical cap, wool inside, the outer surface painted with a red pigment. The fog froze on it in a transparent layer.

He was used to walking in the dark and fog and in snow storms, too. His father and uncles had told him that no man could walk in a straight line without seeing. Everyone had a stronger or longer leg, one over the other, and walking blind you'd gradually swing away from that side. Your master leg stepped just that much longer than its mate. He knew his leader leg was his right, and after he'd gone fifty paces he shifted direction slightly back toward it, allowing for his natural drift to the left. He did this again twice more, and then he began looking out for his signs. He'd marked his hole with three stones and a standing branch.

It didn't surprise him or even really worry him when he couldn't find it straight away. The whole world was down to just a small circle around him, but unless he made a huge mistake and walked southeast down the length of the lake, he'd come to shore eventually. Then he'd find another of his landmarks and try again. Or he'd sit down and wait for the fog to clear. He had time.

It took almost half an hour of casting around, but he found it, finally. There were his stones, and the stick, too. Blown down, but still there. He used it to break the ice within the hole, formed just since yesterday. He spread out his bag, weighted it with one of the stones in case a wind came up, and then stood with his spear pointing down into the hole. He waited, calm and ready. Anything that moved in the water was a target.

The world had been quiet to this point. But now a low sound began, over his left shoulder. It was soft and muted, coming from a long way off and making a gentle, constant moan. He listened with concern, distracted slightly from his concentration. It rose steadily, and although he felt no wind, he hunched his shoulders. He felt colder.

Suddenly and on its own authority, his arm moved, throwing the spear down into the black water. A shriek added itself to the moaning sound, and he yanked the spear back out, bare of any catch. He turned toward the sound ...

Alice came awake. She was cold, even under the comforter, and the foggy ice was still in her mind. Not far away, a train sounded again, crossing another street in the dark. She'd kicked one foot out from under the covers, and it felt as cold as if she'd been standing on the ice, on the Loch of Stenness, trying to catch fish with a Neolithic spear. .

She stretched and sighed and slipped carefully out of bed. Jackie was asleep, breathing quietly. The clock said four-eighteen. As softly as she could, Alice groped for her robe and a pair of slippers. She knew the symptoms already. The train had interrupted a dream, but the dream itself had put an end to sleep. She slipped out of the bedroom and felt her way in the dark to the room they shared as an office. She turned on a low lamp, leaving the ceiling light off, and powered on her laptop. She sat down and waited as it booted up, but when it had, she still sat, staring at the screen.

This was the fourth or fifth time she'd dreamed about the site, the structures and artifacts coming out of the ground at the Ness of Brodgar. It was in the middle of the Orkney Islands, thirty miles north of the northernmost tip of Scotland, as old as Stonehenge or even older, certainly a settlement, maybe a religious center. People were there, living in that stark landscape, making walls and structures, in the last phase of the stone age, three thousand, maybe as long as five thousand years ago. She'd only been there once, physically, but her life was wrapped up with it. When she wasn't teaching undergraduates the difference between lithics and ceramics and not to put your Marshalltown trowel in your back pocket and then sit on it, she lived in that place. She read papers, published and unpublished, draft and finished. She stared at images of material coming out of the squares. She looked for funding. She recruited volunteers. But at the back of it all, there was a subtle kind of fear.

What if the grand question never was answered? What if they dug and measured and dated for the rest of their lives and never found out *why*? *Why* were the people there? Were they running from something? Or withdrawing from something? Did they have a need to be away, in a place that was terribly hard to reach, hard to find? And the walls they built: protection? Against whom?

Professional archeology trained you to steer away from grand models. Late in your career, when you were a few years away from Professor Emeritus, you might try to pull things together, try to write a chronology of the Anasazi, for example, and hint at an answer to where, if anywhere, they went. You might steel yourself, buckle on your body armor, and suggest that perhaps the Clovis people weren't the first Americans. But a newly-made PhD didn't take on unification or dispersion theories or even really talk about them. Something about that frightened her. It was faintly terrifying that she might have to carry on with all of this detail forever, checking off small things that could be known and all of it at the expense of whatever it was she might come to believe.

And then Gerald came back to mind. She had trouble not thinking of him as "poor Gerald" now, someone to whom something terribly bad had happened. Jackie's mother's friend, Mr. MacArthur, hadn't been reassuring. What Alice dreaded most was the chance of never knowing, always wondering about him.

The Sun Bear and the Northern Palm Squirrel

"Yeah, Douglas, this is MacArthur," said Mac. He wondered what Langton's old boss wanted.

"Ah, hi, Mac," Sergeant Douglas sounded hesitant. There could be several reasons for that, Mac thought. "Listen, uh, how you feelin' these days?"

"I like to say 'stable'. Or 'no news is good news'. Nothing new happening. Thanks for asking."

"Sure. Yeah, good to hear it. I was callin' to see if you were interested ... you know, were able to ah, talk to some of our folks."

"Talk?" Mac asked. "Like what? A deposition?" The excessive force business jumped to mind.

"What? No, no. Nothin' like that. I mean consult, I guess. Give some opinions on, ah, a couple of cases we got goin'."

"I can't really take any money for it, you know."

"Yeah, I know. That kinda sucks, I guess."

"Makes perfect sense. The Department's already paying me. Or their insurance is. They pay me to sit home and be sick. And I do a damn good job of it."

"Ok, I see. I guess that's right. But you used to talk to, you know, advise Detective Langton ..."

"Yeah, I did." For some reason, Mac was getting angry. "And while we're on the topic, I didn't have anything to do with her leaving. The only advice I ever gave her was about how to figure out who done it. And she got to be really good at it. Now she's gonna go put it to use where she'll get paid what she's worth ..." He stopped. "*Where did that come from?*" he wondered.

"Oh, no, listen Mac. Nobody thought that. That's not what I'm talkin' about at all. All I'm sayin' is that we're in a jam, sort of. Burke's got a lot of stuff to work on, and ..."

Burke, thought Mac. Of course. "So you want me to work with Louie Burke?"

"Well, yeah. You know. He's, ah, snowed under. And we gotta fill Langton's position, but ... "

"Right. And that's not gonna happen tomorrow."

"Right. So, if maybe he could talk you through some of it? He's got an idea he wants to ..."

"Burke has an idea?"

The conversation wound up predictably. Mac wasn't going to say no; the feeling of being not quite yet useless was intensely pleasant. Burke was a downside of the deal, but at least he'd be a *tabula rasa*. Whatever Mac could manage to teach him would amount to more than the boy had now. Unusually for MacArthur, he let that assessment go unquestioned. Most of the time he'd relieve his various frustrations by an absolute characterization of someone: "*He's an idiot. She's a moron.*" Then his contrary side would kick him under the psychological table, and he'd admit, privately, that the person in question might not be a *complete* waste of oxygen. But this time, with reference to Burke, it didn't happen.

As it turned out, Louie Burke didn't so much have an idea about either of two crimes, but a tiny fragment of witness-supplied information that suggested a connection, at least to him. This was so fascinating to him that he'd told Douglas about it and said that he, Burke, was going to set everything else aside and work on it. Douglas had not been supportive of that plan, and a day later, Burke found himself drinking his usual afternoon beverage – some kind of bottled tea drink -- on MacArthur's couch.

Burke could talk almost endlessly on any topic that interested him, although his narrative style was essentially a mind map. He leapt from point to point in a way that reflected his understanding of things but usually baffled his audience. And outside of work, his interests were almost exclusively related to online gaming. Recently, he'd managed to battle his way to the twelfth degree ranking of a character called "Snorq" in the game of Satanic Sychosis. This achievement had required him to destroy his way from a lovingly rendered post-apocalyptic version of Cincinnati, all the way to a demonic headquarters and stolen starship chop-shop on a planet hidden behind Saturn. He was now trying to find the right weapon – Mac thought he said "Laser Sawzall", but he might have misheard it – which would let him hew his way through a ferrochrome version of Hadrian's Wall and save civilization from an evil being.

"An evil being?" asked Mac, trying to be polite.

"Yeah, he rides this giant, two-wheel thing. He uses a hammer like Thor. His war name is Schnozniak."

"Are there any women in these things?"

That stopped Burke in his tracks. "Wow. I don't know. I mean, there are girls playing, but ..."

"Yeah, but are there any female characters, anybody you'd recognize as female, good or evil?"

"No. No, not really. Some people complained about that, I think. But the programmers said it was too hard."

"Too hard?"

"Yeah, to ,like, program women."

Mac let it drop. He didn't care about computer games, and he only cared very, very slightly about Burke. He wanted to hear about the cases, point out a few elementary mistakes that Burke would have already made, and offer suggestions on how to avoid making more of them. Then, a nap. His joints hurt, his eyes were dried out and sore, and his lower back was beginning to be painful from sitting when it really wanted to be lying down. "So Douglas said you've got a couple of assaults to figure out?"

"Yeah, well, there's the shooting over on the west side and the beat-down over here ..."

"What do you mean, 'over here'?" asked Mac. If anybody was beating-down anybody in his neighborhood, he wanted to know about it.

"You know, east side. Observatory, on campus."

Apparently Burke had decided that if he stood at his desk at the AAPD, facing north, anything on his left was west side and anything to the right was east. That was geographically but not colloquially true; Observatory was definitely not on the "east side". Mac decided to let that go, however, and try to get on with it. "Okay, so just walk me through what we know about 'em." In his disconnected way, Burke summarized the kneecapping of Deano and the mysterious woman who wasn't an assault victim. He finished by laying out his theory.

101

"And, see, both of the subjects were women, and they both had ski masks on!"

Burke was in many ways an idiot, but even he had some ability to sense other people's reactions. His sergeant had not been complementary about this particular insight, and he expected Mac to shoot it down, too. Instead, Mac just looked at him.

"Okay, and that's the sum of what we know? Witnesses, physical stuff, tracks, blood, statements of the victims? Do we know anything else?"

"I think ..."

Mac cut him off. "Hold on. One thing about me: when I use the word *know*, I mean something you're sure of. Not hunches or theories. Facts."

"Oh, okay." Burke was uncertain if he understood. "Yeah, I guess that's what we know."

"All right. Now, let's look at what we might *believe* about it. About the cases. For example, you believe they're related?"

"Well, yeah. I mean, you got two women, wearing ski masks, assaulting guys."

"Okay. What about the guys? The victims? Any connections?"

"Um, no, not that anybody's seen."

"One was a druggie, right? A street dealer?" Mac asked. "And the other one ... ?"

"He was a perv. He had two cases of groping girls on campus already. "

"Women," said Mac.

"What?"

"Women. Not girls, not unless they were kids."

"Oh. Okay." *"Sounds like the Sergeant"*, Burke thought. *"Use this word, don't use that word. Jeez."* "He was grabbing butts on State Street."

"Whose butts?"

"Girl ... women's," Burke said.

"Okay, work on that. You'll sound more professional." *Or at least less like an undergraduate*. "So they're both moderately bad guys. Was the groper in the news at all?"

"In the news?"

"Yeah. Would somebody know about him, know his name?"

"I guess."

"That's something we can *know*," Mac pointed out. We can find that out. And we can find out if any of the groping victims were locals or visitors. If they were working out or doing kick boxing or going to a dojo ... or if they know somebody who was. And once we know things like that, we might believe that your assault victim was decoyed."

"You mean somebody knew he might be hanging out in the cemetery?"

"Yup. I mean we might *believe* that. We wouldn't know it, but it might be a theory we could play with."

"That'd be kind of ... slick, I guess. Complicated. Just for a little butt-pinching."

"That's how you see it. *You* believe it was just a little butt-pinching. Somebody else might see it differently."

Burke looked puzzled. "So you think ..."

"I don't think anything much yet. There's too much I don't know. But while we're having wild ideas, ask yourself this. If – I said *if* – we imagine the woman on Observatory is someone who takes sexual violence very seriously, seriously enough to decoy a perv and whip his ass ... do we think that same person might be just as pissed off at drug dealers?"

"Okay, yeah, so ... you think I'm right about it?"

Mac struggled not to sigh. "It doesn't matter if I *think* one thing or something else. This isn't an election. You don't get votes for your ideas. You want an example?"

"Um, sure." Burke didn't really want one, but he couldn't think of a way to say "no".

Mac leaned back and tried to ease his vertebrae. "We had a homicide, once. A while ago. It wasn't my case, but we all knew about it. There was a kid, good basketball player, I guess. That's what they said, anyway. Good grades. After he was dead, people said a lot of nice things about him. Church family and all that stuff."

Mac looked closely at Burke. He couldn't tell if he was just listening or if he was actually trying to imagine an upstanding young man with a preppy look and some family money. "He and another guy had an apartment, and the roommate comes home and finds him dead. Hit on the head with something hard. Some money and a computer stolen." Burke seemed to be paying attention.

"So what our guys did was, they went over the recent burglaries in studentville. Seemed obvious: door unlocked, thief thinks nobody's home, victim resists, gets clobbered. And they arrested a guy from out of town. Hispanic kid from down river. He had a couple of priors, B and E and an assault, and somebody placed him in town here that day. He said he didn't do it, but duh." He looked straight at Burke. "Sound reasonable?"

"Yeah, I suppose. I mean, you'd need more than that, but it's a start, anyway."

"A start, right. Lasted about two days. Then the roommate comes in, falling apart. He did it. They had a relationship, and our victim wanted out. His family wanted him to go into one of those damn gay-cure programs and get straight. So they had a fight, and his lover hit him with a sauce pan."

All Burke could think of to say was "Wow."

"People felt bad about that."

"Yeah, they grabbed the wrong kid."

"No, that happens. They felt bad about ... " Mac paused. What he meant to say was that *he* felt bad. Like everybody else, domestic violence hadn't occurred to him. You have two guys sharing a student apartment, they're not lovers. They're just roommates. Must have been some predatory little creep from out of town. Wrong side of the tracks. Wrong side of US-23. *Over there*. "They missed the story," he said. "They made assumptions. That was what embarrassed people." Later, maybe later, he'd try raising Burke's social consciousness. For now, he left it at "*try not to assume anything*".

"But how is that ... how's that like what I'm looking at?"

Mac was mildly pleased. That was a more intelligent question than most of Burke's.

"If you find somebody who fits our little scheme, don't go nuts with it. Say you find a woman who reported an assault by our Observatory street jackass. And it turns out she's got some mixed martial arts chops. And maybe she comes from some place with real drug problems. That's probably too good to be true. You go lean on her and then you find out that the perv's wife's sister did the beating. And she's from some town in the UP where they can't spell heroin."

"So I'm screwed ..."

"Maybe. Your subject didn't stomp the butt-pincher. But you could still go back and talk to her casually about all the heroin in the community. See if she reacts, see what she says. Just because somebody isn't a suspect in one thing doesn't mean they aren't up to something else."

When Burke left MacArthur's house, the dogs saw him to the door. They were polite about it, but when he was gone, they stood and looked rather pointedly at Mac. Snacker glanced toward the kitchen and then back. Both wagged their tails slowly and in the same rhythm. "What?" said MacArthur. "Dinner time, is it?" He looked at his watch; it was, in fact, 4:40. "You're right, as usual."

He led the way into the kitchen and dished out a homemade blend of meat and vegetables. As the retired guy, he was the one with time to make up batches of MacArthur's Own Secret Recipe Dog Food, reflecting the family belief that anything commercial was probably toxic. The Shepherds seemed to appreciate it. While they ate, Mac watched them and thought in a meditative way about what their mental processes might be. It was calming; in the effort to be a dog himself, he forgot for a moment about Louie Burke and his avenging demoness theory.

But the spell didn't last. A thought kept coming back, and it was a thought that had first arrived as he prepared for the little chat he and Burke had just had. What if we actually have *three* cases, not two, of an angry woman working out her anger? Three cases: Deano the druggie, the campus perv, and ... Rusty the hit and run boy? He couldn't stop himself from wondering what Jeri Klein's recent duty schedule looked like.

As for Burke, he was uncomfortable, too, as he headed back to the Department. He had a big to-do list and a lot to ponder. He understood, partly, Mac's distinction between knowing and believing, but it seemed sort of philosophical for police work. And both of his victims were bad guys, anyway. Serves 'em right, he thought. "*And I gotta dig through a lot of stuff.*" He started running over the stuff, trying to sort it out and decide what he needed to know. "*I know it was a woman, anyway. I know that.*" He stopped. Something uncomfortable drifted across his mind. "*I think I know that. Do I know it?*" An ill-defined spot above his right eyebrow started to hurt. "*How the hell do I know what I really know?*" Not too far away, Bertrand Russell's essence smiled.

Canis lupus familiaris **The Dogs**

Mac was nervous. He didn't know anybody in the Grosse Pointe Park Department of Public Safety; he didn't know anybody in Grosse Pointe Park. Alice couldn't tell him the name of the person she spoke to. *Hell*, he thought, *this is going to be great.* "*Hi, I'm an old, retired cop in Ann Arbor ... yes, that's where the college is. And all the liberals, yeah. Listen, a friend's daughter's partner's cousin lives in your city, and ...*" He'd had to field a few calls like that himself, over the years, and the caller had invariably been confused, drunk, and / or an idiot. He wasn't sure how he'd play this one. Having lunch with Jenn Langton once in a while and acting like the wise old guru was one thing. Getting into a gun fight with people who might have been drug dealers or arms dealers or antique dealers for all anyone ever found out, that he could live with. Nobody'd shot him, and (probably) he hadn't shot anybody else. But this ...

The main problem was: missing adults, apparently not suffering from anything diagnosable, were a very touchy thing. As everyone had been telling Alice, people like that had a right to go missing. It was embarrassing enough for the actual police when they found someone who didn't want to be found. For Mac, as a free-lance philosopher and caffeine addict, to stumble on this Temple guy in his little love nest or in a cult or in jail somewhere could be more than embarrassing. It might even be illegal.

As a start, he assembled the essential tools: a large coffee and the Internet. He began with a search for Fisher Gerald Temple, and he got little enough. Temple was on LinkedIn, and it said the usual things. He'd been born, went to college, got a degree, had a couple of jobs, hadn't apparently died yet. All but one of the jobs had been elsewhere; just the most recent one ("2012 to present") was in Ann Arbor. Some company called FastFF. Mac knew most of the bigger employers in town, but this place, no. Temple's profile didn't say anything about having left the company, "seeking new opportunities", or anything like that.

He looked up the company website, saw that it was some kind of financial thing, and found Temple listed as Chief Financial Officer. *"So they don't keep their site up to date, or they don't think he's gone anywhere,"* Mac thought. A third possibility occurred to him: *"Or they haven't noticed."* He hauled out his phone and tried the company's general number. It took three voice mail choices to get an actual human.

"Yes, good morning. I'd like to speak to Mr. Temple, please."

"I'm sorry, Sir," said the voice on the other end , immediately. "He's out of the office."

"Oh, that's too bad. I wanted to tell him the contract goes through this afternoon." Mac had years of experience in lying his way past Admins.

"Would you like his voice mail?" Standard second move, pawn to D6.

"Well, is there someone else I could talk to?" This was only sometimes successful. The obstacle-employee has been given the notion (whether he believes it or not) that the call might be important. If it gets blown off, the Admin might be in trouble. If he lets it go to someone else, it might be politically bad, as in: only Mr. Temple is supposed to know about whatever the caller has in mind. Unfortunately, this Admin was nobody's fool.

"You'd have to speak with one of the executives, and they're all in a meeting now. I'd be happy to take a personal message for Mr. Temple." Pawn takes pawn.

"Ah, all right. Tell him that Ms. Graves' attorney called. My number is ..." He gave his own number. He usually didn't claim to be somebody's lawyer, but he was winging this one. He thanked the young man and hung up. Stalemate, but he did learn something: *Temple's not just ignoring Alice, he's blowing off business calls, too. Or he has a really experienced Admin.*

All right, then. Same game, different opponent. Mac found the website of the Grosse Point Park Cops. It was a sub-link from the city's home page, and a bit of clicking found him a list of personnel. Mac scanned down the thirty or so names, looking for anyone familiar. He got past the As and Bs quickly, and then he stopped short. "*Son of a bitch!*" he said aloud. There were only two officers with C last names, and one of them was Brian Colton.

The last Mac heard from or about a Brian Colton, he was the canine handler at the Sturgis, Michigan, Police Department. Goose's old partner. The one who'd called Mac when Goose more or less resigned and decided he wanted to be a house dog. Unless there were two Brian Coltons in southern Michigan law enforcement, this was almost certainly somebody he knew. He went to his phone again.

This time, he got through much more quickly. Colton was due to clock in shortly, the desk person said, but she'd heard about Goose, and she promised to give Colton a message as soon as he showed up. In fact, Mac had only been off the phone a few minutes when he got the call back.

"Mr. MacArthur? Brian Colton. Hey, I got a message here that says "*Goose called.*" Is he okay?"

"Hey, Brian. Thanks for calling back. Yeah, Goose says *Hi*. He's fine, fat and happy. Um, I got a weird question for you, though. You moved from Sturgis, I guess?"

"Yeah. This was more money. You knew we had a baby, right? Turns out, they're expensive."

"Yeah, I bet they are. So, here's the deal: a friend of a friend asked me to check out something for her. You know who'd be working on a missing person thing in your shop?"

The events that followed were unusual, unusual in the sense that they didn't go through any kind of documented process. The city had a very small department, a flat organization with mostly do-ers, not many bosses, and a modest budget. In particular, they had no canine team. What they did have was a good set of cooperative agreements with the small neighboring cities. In extreme situations, they'd also ask Detroit, the State Police, the County, and sometimes the FBI for help, but that was usually a case of going hat in hand and taking what was offered.

The Temple missing person thing (as Colton called it), hadn't yet come up to the level of an investigation. That didn't mean it hadn't been discussed, and there were even some handwritten notes, laying out what might have to happen if ... But nothing formal. When the Chief, a man in charge of both Police and Fire issues, heard from Colton that a) somebody from Ann Arbor was interested in a local guy gone walkabout and that b) the caller was a known good guy, not a nut, and c) he had a trained police dog he could bring to the party, the Chief didn't throw Brian out of his office. Instead, he called the guys in Ann Arbor. He knew a couple of them, and after a few short "Who is this MacArthur guy and what is he up to?" conversations, he told Colton to let him run Goose around the possible victim's neighborhood. "It can't really hurt, I guess."

That was Monday. There was some phone calling to be done, but by Wednesday, Mac and the dogs had a date, first with Colton, then with Mrs. Temple and a piece of Gerald's clothing, and then with the streets of the city. Mac got up early, got the dogs fed and in the truck, and laid in coffee supplies for the trip. The baristas were curious, but all Mac said was "Takin' 'em for a little walk." He wasn't comfortable with this deal, and he didn't want to talk about it. Colleen knew, obviously, but otherwise, he was treating it as a more or less covert mission.

It was fifty miles, almost exactly, by the shortest route, and that path was through some of the nastier freeways. It cut across the roads into Detroit like cutting across the spokes of a wheel, and they were leaving a bit too late to miss work traffic. The drive was just as bad as Mac expected, although the dogs cooperated by curling up on their respective seats and going to sleep. They missed the trucks that merged on too slowly and then made up for it by going too fast. They didn't experience the manic white collar folks in their sedans and SUVs, juggling phones and breakfast burritos, putting on makeup or trying to shave. They didn't see the Bubbas in immense pickup trucks or the Millennials in Fits and Smart Cars. Mac got it all, though, and by the time they filtered down into Grosse Point Park, he was exhausted and angry. He didn't do this kind of driving much, and he felt the same "*What have we done?*" distaste for humanity that he did in supermarkets. He comforted himself by reflecting that he'd had to keep his eyes on the road. He hadn't had a chance to see the surroundings.

Brian Colton greeted them and got an enthusiastic "Hello!" from Goose. Snacker didn't remember him and was more reserved, but she knew a dog man when she met one. They got in Colton's patrol car, and he took them for a quick drive around what had been Gerald Temple's neighborhood. They started with his block of Audubon Road and then did a square around the adjoining streets. Colton talked about the town in general, seeing it as a new arrival from a very different community. Mac just watched the houses. It wasn't selling season, but still he was surprised at how few seemed to be for sale. All were higher-end places, diverse designs, mostly older. In fact, he saw only a couple of recent builds.

Colton confirmed it. "The new houses are all places where something burned or maybe there was a vacant lot. Not many of those." Mac thought about that. On Temple's home street, the houses were uniformly set back from the curb. One street west, they had longer, curving driveways and a more luxurious look. They were clearly a decade newer.

They finished half their tour, went east on Jefferson past Audubon one block, then back north again to finish a square search. Here, the seventies construction blended with the newer and more pretentious homes. "So this is all pretty much the same period?" Mac asked.

"Yeah. Yeah, I think they built all of this pretty much at once."

"Ah." Mac doubted that. They finished the drive and stopped at Temple's house. "Any sense of the kind of people in the neighborhood? All commuters, mostly gone during the day? That sort of thing?"

"Well ... I guess, yeah. I mean, nobody's really around now, right?" It was 10:30 on a weekday. "And not a lot of cars parked on the street, either."

"*Lot of garages, though*," Mac thought, but he said nothing. "*This is an opportunity to shut up*." He wanted Colton to talk, not to listen. He wanted to find out how much the new guy on the force had been told about the town and its people, how much he'd been able to pick up quickly on his own. So far, it didn't seem as though he knew all that much, and that little, unscientific, shaky piece of intelligence would help Mac decide how much he could trust any socio-economic information he might hear from the local cops. "*The local cops*," he thought. "*I sound like the FBI*."

So far, he hadn't heard much about the neighborhood at all. Michigan was two months into a nasty winter, and here people seemed to be either holed up or off at work. Colton had driven eight blocks, slowly and looking carefully around, and they hadn't seen a soul except for one woman in a car. He guessed at the people here: probably affluent, maybe not full-blown wealthy. They live here, work somewhere else. Mostly white. The sidewalks and driveways were cleared with a precision and consistency that pointed at professional help, not old Dad out there in the cold with a shovel. He imagined it in the summer, with the streets congested with lawn service trucks. Yeah, maybe not a place where you saw much of your random neighbors.

"What was the wife's name, again?" Mac asked.

"Uh, Alison. Alison Temple."

"Okay. Want to have a chat with her?"

They left the dogs in the patrol car and walked up to the door. Audubon Street was lined with a mix of trees, and some of them blocked their associated houses. The Temples' place was one of those, with a large, older maple in the easement and two newer trees growing up fast beside it. Even though the leaves were long gone, Mac recognized catalpas; his own street was almost roofed over with them. Through the bare branches you could see a symmetrical, cone shaped spruce and a cheesy-looking "Greek" facade. The driveway went up the south side, curved, and disappeared. If there was a garage, it was somewhere behind the house.

Alison Temple was five-seven or so, a little heavier than she probably wanted to be, and not especially happy. She'd reported her husband missing ten days ago, and nothing had happened. She was, she said, beginning to be seriously concerned. Mac filed that away for later; "*He's ten days AWOL and she's "beginning" to be concerned?*"

Brian said the usual, conciliatory things connected with adult missing persons, and explained that the department had arranged for Mr. MacArthur here to help out. "Mr. MacArthur has a professionally-trained law enforcement canine," he said, which was true enough. If Mrs. Temple assumed that Mac was a consultant instead of an old, beat up retiree from another city, that was her problem. They asked for the usual sample of Gerald's clothing – always carefully referring to him as "her

114

husband" or "Mr. Temple," never as "the victim" — and promised to return when they'd had a chance to canvass the neighborhood. "Canvass" always sounded better than "search", especially when there was no real expectation that they'd find anything.

Snacker wasn't any kind of a tracking dog, unless you were looking for squirrels or edible detritus, but it wouldn't have been practical to leave her behind. Mac took her leash and Colton took Goose, giving him a white short-sleeved T-shirt of Gerald's to smell. Goose sniffed it without much interest, but then the details of this particular game started to come back to him. He spent a few minutes on the garage and the back yard, then trotted out to the sidewalk.

Colton let him look up and down the block, and when he didn't select one direction over another, encouraged him to head south. They went slowly, stopping and starting (a mode that Mac's hips and knees objected to strongly). They looked under a parked car, sniffed and rejected a storm drain, and lingered around numerous garbage bins. At the end of the block, they went east, then south again. It was solidly residential, solidly respectable. There were no opium dens, no brothels, no taverns in which a man could be drugged and sold into slavery. The dogs seemed to think it was just another walk in a fairly uninteresting part of the world. Colton was about to suggest that their feet might be getting cold (overtly meaning the dogs' feet, but including his own as well), when Goose suddenly stopped. He back-tracked a few feet and turned up a driveway. Mac noticed that he'd chosen one of the few houses with a "For Sale" sign.

Goose had experienced a sort of canine epiphany. He remembered his training, and that training seemed, as he recalled it, to involve a game in which the object was to find a hiding human. Sometimes you found the human by smelling them, sometimes they made a noise, but almost always they were running away or hiding. And humans, he'd learned, usually tried to hide by getting behind or under things, into places where they couldn't be seen. What he smelled now was nothing like the T-shirt, but it was obviously a human, and since he couldn't see the human, *voila*, it must be hiding! He led Colton up the driveway and around the back of the house. He followed the scent directly to a pile of snow beside the back door, and he sat down. He pointed at the pile with his nose. He looked at Brian, then back at the snow.

Mac and Snacker caught up, and Mac made her sit, too. Brian handed him Goose's leash, and stepped forward. Goose yipped slightly in approval. Colton bent down, hesitated, and tried to brush the snow aside. It was frozen, and he had to cup his hand and dig. He cleared away a few square inches, looked carefully, then felt the thing he'd uncovered. He stood up.

"We better make a call," he said. "It's a body."

The Swift Fox, The Marbled Cat, the Red Panda, and The Sun Bear

"I could get used to this," Jenn thought. She was sitting or actually reclining in a lounge chair on a balcony. She was wearing khaki shorts and a loose shirt, and her bare feet were just getting slightly pink in the afternoon sun. From left to right, Cruz Bay was a semi-circle of blue water. The harbor was about half full of boats, and the ferry from Redhook was coming in. It was somewhere around seventy-five degrees, and the only thing that needed analysis and decision was dinner. She gave a grateful thought to Colleen MacArthur; Mac's wife had suggested Saint John in the US Virgins as a slow, relaxed honeymoon, and she'd been right. The MacArthurs even had a favorite place to stay and favorite restaurants and a favorite jeep rental place ... and it had all worked out. She was

between jobs, between places, getting used to being married again. Perfect.

Her phone rang. Those old nervous twitches kicked back in, but only momentarily. It was the good daughter, the newly-favorite kid, the one with a nice stable partner and a place in Ann Arbor.

"Hi, Jackie."

"Oh, hi, Mom. How's the island?"

"Just about, well, paradise, I'd have to say. What's up, besides the thermostat?" Per the Internet, it was twelve degrees in southeastern Michigan.

"Nothing, really. I didn't want to, um, interrupt ... you on your ..."

"Honeymoon. Hang on a minute, will you?" Jenn took the phone a few inches from her mouth and said, loudly "Oh, Andy, not the gorilla suit again! I'm on the phone!" Andy was, in fact, in the shower and unable to hear any of the conversation. Two thousand linear miles away, Jackie blushed and giggled. "Now, what's on your mind?"

"Oh, I just wanted to say thanks for getting Alice in touch with Mr. MacArthur."

"So they talked?"

"Yeah, and he's going to go to Grosse Pointe something ... where Alice's cousin lived, you know ... and take his dogs and see if they can track anything."

"Really?" Jenn was immediately on edge. "Like when?"

"Um, now, I think. I think he was going to go today."

"All right, then. Thanks ... ah, thanks for letting me know. So you think that's happening already, right?"

"Yeah. Maybe. I think that's what Alice said. She said he knew somebody in the Police over there."

Jenn could hear the shower turn off. The buzzword "*awkward*" came to mind. She exchanged a few more pleasantries with Jackie, and managed to get her off the phone before Andy came out of the bathroom. They'd already been together long enough to read major if not subtle changes in each other. "What's up?" he said.

"I'm afraid I might have ... meddled," she said.

"Meddled how?"

"You told me about that case you had going? The dirty finance company?"

"Yeah?"

"And how they had one CFO die and another one kind of drop out of sight?"

"Yes." He was beginning to feel uneasy.

"And I said, oh, that's funny. Just like Jackie's Alice — her cousin is a financial guy and he's missing."

"I remember."

"Well, before that ... seriously, *before* you told me about your case ... I pointed Alice at MacArthur."

"At Mac?"

"Yeah. And I think Mac is stomping around in Grosse Pointe Park right now, with his dogs, looking for bodies or clues or something."

Andy froze for just a second. His right hand, well behind the kitchen island and out of sight, clenched and unclenched involuntarily. He drew in a breath as quietly as he could and let it out again. "Oh, I see. Okay. Thanks for letting me know. Do you want the shower now?"

"Sure. Sure, I'll just take a quick shower now."

"Fine. I can, um, return some calls, and then ... dinner."

"Right, dinner."

It was a quarter after five in Ann Arbor. Mac answered his phone.

"Mr. MacArthur?"

"Yes, who's this?"

"This is Agent Corcoran with the FBI."   "*What the hell?*," thought Mac.

One hundred and twenty seconds later, he hung up. "*What the fuck?!?*" thought Mac.

In his office, well inside the FBI building and with no views at all of Detroit's Mack Avenue and Cass, Agent Corcoran added a note to the record of an on-going investigation. "*Contacted ex-AAPD Police Officer named above and advised him not to have further contact with any agencies or subjects involved in this investigation*." He shook his head and looked back at the last report filed. His colleague, Agent Patel, had written:

"Summary information from site surveillance at 1532 9½ Mile Road, Eastpointe, MI. Periodic surveillance of Apartment 232 at the above address was carried out during the period 2013 11 26 through 2014 01 27 (date of disappearance of subject 07). Based on prior information, subject 07 (Fisher Gerald Temple) was known to have leased this apartment a month before surveillance began, and to have visited it, on average, twice a week, on Tuesdays and Thursdays, arriving between 8:00 PM and 8:30 PM, staying inside for approximately 2 hours, and upon leaving, driving directly back to his home. During this period, the investigation made no attempt to gain access to the apartment or to obtain electronic intelligence.

Subject was always alone on arrival, there was no indication (lights, etc.) of anyone being in the apartment when he arrived. No one else entered the apartment while he was there, and he always left alone. Subject's mobile phone neither made nor received calls or text messages during this time. (Turned off?)

On three dates in late November and early December, another vehicle was observed in the parking lot adjacent to Apartment 232, and the single male, African-American occupant was observed engaged in behavior that was judged to be surveillance. He was identified via vehicle registration as Henry Cooper, licensed Private Investigator, with a home and office address in Sterling Heights, MI. After Subject 07 disappeared, Mr. Cooper was contacted, and he stated and demonstrated with documentation that he had been retained by the wife(subject 22) of subject 07 to carry out an inquiry into subject 07's absences on the nights noted above, and to report his opinion as to

120

whether subject 07 was involved in a relationship with one or more other persons (unspecified). Mr. Cooper provided the investigation with a copy of his report (linked below) to subject 22, the summary of which is that subject 07's activities in the apartment were unknown, but that they did not involve any other party. Cooper was advised to decline any further requests from any party regarding subjects 07 and 22."

"Our CFO guy rents an apartment and goes there four hours a week and does nothing?" Corcoran thought. *"And then he drops out of sight?"* He turned the page.

"After subject 07 was determined to be unaccounted for, the investigation obtained access to the apartment and conducted a search. It was found to be partially empty; there were four rooms in all, a kitchen, a bed room, a bathroom, and a living room. The kitchen held no food or drinks except for a bottle of water. Stove and refrigerator were disconnected, and there were no cooking, eating, or cleaning utensils or supplies. The bed room had no furniture and the closet was empty except for the clothes described below. The living room was furnished with what appeared to be reproduction furniture, lighting, and decorations representing the Victorian era. (An expert has confirmed this.)

The clothes in the bed room closet appeared to be two different sets of period costumes, suggesting, again, the Victorian era or more generally the late nineteenth century (also confirmed by an expert). Both sets of clothing were male pattern suits, including a jacket or coat, trousers, and shirts. One pair of shoes, also of costume quality and of the same period, were found. One of the jackets was traced to a theatrical supply company in Bloomfield Hills, MI; the others were unlabeled. Any effort to trace the clothes by contacting vendors is being held up until the main investigation concludes."

"*No books, no TV*" thought Corcoran, "*Or else I'd think he just went there to get away from his wife.*" The FBI was making an effort to find out just what kind of crap FastFF corporation was up to, and it wasn't going well. Two CFOs in two months, one kills himself totaling his car, one just drops off the planet. And no clear idea whether the company was really breaking the law at all. A regulation or too, absolutely, but every bank in sight did that. "*Including,*" he thought, "*The one I use.*" He shook his head again. It would be great to have Patel back and pulling his weight. Corcoran's own honeymoon had been fifteen years back, and he had a hard time remembering it.

The Barefoot Weasel and the Lionesses

Like most smaller American cities, Ann Arbor didn't invest in an overall, official surveillance system. So many businesses and institutions had their own security cameras in place that it hardly seemed useful to spend money on a civic network. Plus, it dodged the inevitable privacy debate. But in MacArthur's years of investigation, he seemed to keep getting cases where the crime or the hypothetical crime took place in that one block that didn't have coverage. Or there was a camera running, but it was old and took such crummy video that all you could see was one genderless, raceless, unidentifiable person punching another. And so he began keeping a list of where cameras were and where they were pointed. He graded them for quality, too, when he remembered to note it. After a while, the list moved from his notebook onto a spreadsheet, and it was still there, being updated occasionally, when he left the Department. He turned it over to his supervisor, and the supervisor asked for a volunteer to keep it going. Jeri Klein stepped up.

Mac's idea had been to use the data after the fact. An assault took place, you looked at the list, and you went straight to the business owner or the landlord whose cameras had the best angle on the crime. Jeri had another thought: note the spots where there *weren't* cameras. If you had a surveillance assignment or you just had time to kill, you picked the empty places to watch, knowing that nothing else was covering them. She'd already made one burglary arrest because although there was no video, *she* saw it going down. And another difference: Mac hadn't worried about securing the information; Jeri put a password on the file.

Tonight, she was sitting in her patrol car, actually her patrol SUV. The Department had an Explorer with a police kit, and with the way the winter was shaping up, there'd probably be another one in the next budget cycle. She had no immediate business, and she was using the time to test a theory. The hypothesis was that when the Michigan Theater ran films for an older and more affluent audience – as opposed to students – there was a greater chance of low-end property crime as the crowd left and dispersed to their cars. The immediate areas had two long-established drinking spots for the young and unsocialized; Jeri's belief was that if anyone was going to grab a purse on a cold winter night, the block of Maynard between Liberty and William would be a good place for it. And the purse of an art-film enthusiast, off guard and engrossed in a deconstructionist appreciation of the director's worldview would be an easy purse to snatch. Further, the south half-block of Maynard was a video-free zone, "*dark railroad*" as she liked to call it. She shut the engine off, adhering to a Departmental suggestion that citizens didn't like to see official cars idling, wasting gas. And to spare the battery, she shut off the twelve-volt power, too.

Jeri didn't really believe she was going to save any lives or rebuild society with this sort of intellectualizing, but she preferred to have a reason for doing something, and since there weren't any domestic abuse cases or vandalism calls going, it gave her an excuse to be sitting here, facing north and looking past the entrance to Nickels Arcade, watching the tunnel where the entire street ducked under a parking ramp. At the end of Maynard and just across Liberty, the Michigan's last showing was about to end. In a few minutes, a hundred or so people would leave and head to their cars. The drawback to sitting and watching was, of course, that it didn't keep her from thinking. The last month, her thinking had been going down one terrifying path.

The movie audience flowed past, growing and then tapering off. One man saw Klein and looked away nervously. A couple nodded to her. She kept her eyes on the tunnel. If there was going to be any trouble, it would probably start with someone coming out of the beer-soaked sports bar just on the other side. You walked by its door on your way to the elevators in the parking ramp. But nothing happened. She was within a few minutes of moving on, looking for problems in other places, when a last pair of movie-goers came out of the dark quarter-block and walked on toward her. They were two older women, dressed against the cold and walking arm in arm. One of them had a stick. A stick? Jeri looked harder. Yes, it was a hiking staff, not a cane, and she was actually using it, putting weight on it with each step. She seemed used to it, placing it carefully but without needing to look down. They were talking, heads close together, and their breath was trailing back in a small cloud. It was very cold.

They had walked about half the way to Jeri's car when somebody shouted. She didn't get the words, but it was loud and it sounded like a command. The women heard it and turned around, separating from each other. Two young men trotted out of the tunnel toward them. Jeri hit her lights and started to get out of the car.

124

One of the men saw the flashers and tried to stop. He slipped and fell, ten feet from the women. His friend kept coming, his hand reaching out for the purse that one of the women was carrying. The word "Stop!" was queued up in Jeri's larynx, waiting for her to finish breathing in and be ready to shout it. But before she could, the older woman stepped toward the man, shifted her grip on the stick, and whipped it up, left, and across his chest. It caught him under the chin, and he lost his footing. The other man got to his feet and simply ran, back toward Liberty.

Jeri got her command out, as loudly as she could while running and trying not to fall on the poorly-scraped pavement. The man who'd been hit finished falling, landing hard on the sidewalk, right in front of the woman. She was stepping back, reversing the stick and preparing to bring the grip end down on his head. Jeri was nearly there, about to yell again, when the second woman beat her to it.

"Stay on the ground!" She'd dropped back a pace and gone into a Weaver stance, both hands holding a small handgun.

In another two steps, Jeri was beside her, shouting "Stop!" again. Everyone froze. An awkward arrangement of people existed, Jeri and both the women as the base of a triangle, the young man at the apex. No one moved. "I have a concealed carry license," said woman number two.

Jeri made eye contact with the man, and he looked away, staring at the pistol. She shifted to the first woman who returned the look, then glanced at the knob end of her staff, and finally down at the man. She looked back at Jeri and arched her eyebrows. Jeri looked around. There was no one. She said to woman two, "Just put it away." She looked back at the other one and nodded her head slightly. Woman one brought the stick down slanting in toward the boy's face. She hit him precisely on the jaw, breaking it handily and taking a pair of teeth out. Then she stepped back and grounded her staff like an infantryman. The pistol had vanished.

Klein pulled the miscreant up off the sidewalk, spun him around, and put him against the wall of the parking structure. She got his hands behind his back and cuffed before he had enough of his wits back to begin denying things. "I didn't do noth ..." She cut him off by putting the injured side of this face harder against the bricks and carefully listed his rights.

"What ... what did I doooo?" he wailed.

"You're under arrest for simple assault, aggravated assault, resisting arrest, assault on a police officer, use of a weapon in the commission of a felony, and making terroristic threats," she told him quietly and with a tone of assurance.

"What weapon? Assaulted who?! I didn't assault nobody!"

"Where's the knife?" she asked.

"What knife? I didn't have no knife."

"What did he do with the knife?" she asked the women. They were standing there feeling the adrenaline fade. One of them was worrying, trying to remember the legal definition of "brandishing" a pistol.

"What knife?"

"Didn't you see the knife he had?" Jeri asked. There was a pause. "You saw the knife, didn't you?"

The older woman woke up quickly. "Oh, yes. Yes, of course. The knife. He had it in ... his hand."

"Did he throw it down somewhere?"

"I ... didn't see. Yes, he must have thrown it. Maybe into the street."

"She had a gun! She pulled a gun on me!"

"Listen, Sir," said Jeri. "You better just quit lying and stand there. You're in enough trouble as it is."

"But the gun ..."

"I didn't see any gun." Jeri looked straight at woman one. "Do you have a gun?"

"I ... no, I don't have a gun. No gun at all. I don't."

"Yeah, " Jeri said, "I didn't see you have a gun. I just saw you defend yourself with your ... cane."

"My staff. Yes, I had to hit him with my walking staff."

"Would you two like to sit in my car while I get someone to look at the subject? He might need some medical attention."

The comings and goings involved in cleaning up an attempted robbery (they didn't find a knife, and so the weapon charge went away) took far longer than the incident itself. Neither of the women was hurt, and no property had been stolen, but it took a while to get their statements written out. One was a faculty member, the other a retired orthopedic surgeon. Finally, they were given a short ride to their car, and they drove soberly home.

The supervisor read over the charges. "What's this terroristic threats business? They didn't say anything about that."

"Oh, I heard it very clearly," Jeri said. "He said "*Give me that purse or I'll kill you, you dike bitches!*" We could probably make it hate speech, too."

He cocked an eyebrow, skeptically.

"Well, we can drop it if you think so," she said. Her voice was even and professional. "As long as there's still a felony in there, I'm fine."

"Yeah. I guess," he paused. "Too bad there aren't any cameras down here."

The Barefoot Weasel Alone

Jeri Klein sat on the edge of her bed. She was breathing in and out with great and deliberate control, as if she were preparing for a sprint or a leap or a confrontation. *"I can do this,"* she thought. *"I'm strong and confident and prepared."* She didn't often speak directly to herself, but this ritual called for it. It was almost a prayer to a goddess of self-control. *"I am what I have made myself. I am what I have deliberately become."*

She was wearing only a pair of stretch briefs, with legs that came down to mid-thigh. She got up stiffly, and her gate was stiff as she walked to the closet. To one side, where they wouldn't easily be seen, hung her strong clothes. She put them on mechanically, stepping into the loose trousers and then shrugging into the tunic. She buttoned the shirt front and the fly of the pants. Then she bent and put on a pair of boots, fastening them over the trouser cuffs. She put on a broad-brimmed cloth hat.

She stood for another few seconds, staring at the dark closet. Then she turned and walked mechanically into the bathroom. It was dim, and she paused, looking at a shadow person in the mirror. She flicked on the lights, and her reflection snapped into view. She saw someone who might or might not be a woman, wearing old-style tiger stripe camouflage. The person's face was covered in brown and green bands of makeup, with the darker shades concentrated around the eye sockets. She stared into that face and consciously stiffened her back. She breathed in again, breathed out, breathed in once more. She began to unbutton the tunic.

She undid the buttons one at a time from top to bottom. As the shirt opened, she saw her own light brown skin beginning at the top where the camouflage ended and extending downward in a vertical strip, growing wider with each button. When the tunic hung completely open, she paused again, staring at her own eyes. Using her left hand, she pulled the shirt back across her torso. Her right hand moved across and closed around the lower half of her left breast. Two fingertips pressed together.

There was a sensation like ice water at the back of her neck and another feeling like a mixture of heat and pressure at her temples. She blinked hard. "*Oh, god, oh god! It's still there!*" With a dreadful clarity, the small lump stood out against her fingers, just below the nipple. Her hand shook, and a tear slipped down one green painted cheek.

The Lar Gibbon Wakes

The campfire flames flashed and undulated, varying the light. Sometimes the wall of stones to the right was lit, sometimes it disappeared in the darkness. From that side, the wind was blocked, but it shifted, too, coming from the northwest , backing around to the east, whipping branches back and forth, going back again to a steady north gale. A few flakes of snow came with it, sideways, striking her face or vanishing in the fire. As the firelight rose, the fear lifted; when it died down and the circle closed in, so did an uneasiness.

Deep in one of the logs, there was a gap, filled with moisture. The fire heated it, finally, to boiling, and it exploded, sending sparks into the air, making a sharp snapping sound. She pulled her sheepskin cloak closer around her. The fire reached another pocket in the wood, but this time it only made a hole, and the steam rushed out, hissing. It curled away, partly up with the flames, partly off into the dark with the wind.

Far away in the dark, there was a howling sound. The fire snapped again, and she sensed movement on her left. She turned her head, and there was a man standing there, hands at his sides. He wore leggings tied in place, and in the uncertain light the figures painted on them seemed to move. She looked up at his face, but it was still in darkness. She tried to rise, but something kept her from getting up. The wind rushed in suddenly, blowing up the fire and lighting the man's face. It was the face of a wolf! She shouted something in a language she'd never heard, and ...

Her head lolled forward, her neck tired of holding it up. Her eyes opened, and she could see her monitor and the keyboard below it. She blinked hard, twice, and focused on the screen. A site report was still there, overlapping with a grant application in another window. Behind her, a voice said "Your phone was ringing."

Alice looked blankly at the University desk phone, but the voice said, "No, your phone. *Your* phone."

"My phone," Alice said. She bent and picked up her general purpose bag; it was a purse, a backpack, a shopping bag when necessary. It was white canvas with a Celtic design. She fished around in it for her phone.

"You said something. In your sleep," said the voice. "Are you all right?"

"Yes," Alice said. The person in her office was just a graduate student, just there for a semester, no one who had any business knowing she'd fallen asleep, let alone commenting on it. She found the phone, and it told her whose call she'd missed. "Excuse me," she said, and walked out into the corridor.

At a window, ten or fifteen paces away, she stopped and long-pressed 1 to get to voice mail. She looked outside, across campus, seeing sidewalks like trenches, long linear piles of snow on each side. It was a bit after four-thirty, and the sky was already darkening.

"Ah, Ms. Graves. This is Mac MacArthur. Uh, I just wanted to give you a ... give you an idea of how things went in Grosse Pointe. We found ... well, it's good news and bad news, I guess. We went out with my dogs and one of the local police, and we didn't really find anything about your cousin. Nothing, actually. So that's not so good. You might see something in the news about finding a body in Grosse Pointe Park, but don't worry about that. It's not related. It was a young woman. Missing out of Detroit. For a couple of months. I guess that's not good, either, actually ... but again, nothing to do with your cousin."

Alice nodded. She had the habit of responding to people on the phone as if they were present, and sometimes even a voice mail message could get the same reaction.

"I don't think I can really do much more for you on this," the message went on. "But what I think ... I think what I'd do if I were you, is I'd talk to, uh, Jenn Langton ... to Jackie Langton's mother, ah, again, and see what else she might ... think about it. Sorry. Goodbye."

"*Good God!*" Alice thought. "*Good God Almighty.*"

She shut the phone down and walked back toward her desk. The world had slowed down and narrowed while she listened to MacArthur's message. Now it was returning to its usual speed. "*I don't know anything new,*" she thought. "*Nothing has changed.*" And the grant application was still open on her desktop.

The Barefoot Weasel in Repose

Armed robbery in progress, Packard Avenue. Most of the Ann Arbor, U of M, and Washtenaw patrol officers who heard that call felt something between unease and actual fear. Jeri Klein heard it with something on the border of exhilaration, and she accelerated with enough force to slide the rear of the car. She was on Packard, close in, driving past rows of student houses and apartment blocks, but the call was for a location farther out to the east, in one of several blocks of small businesses. There were Asian and Near Eastern markets, small restaurants, a bicycle shop, things that needed reasonable rent to stay in business. She recovered from the slide automatically. Her mind was busy visualizing the specific parking lot, the actual store where someone was committing a strong arm crime, allegedly with a handgun. She knew from the units responding that she wouldn't be the first officer there, but she meant to be the second one.

Jeri blew through six separate traffic signals, driving faster than she should have been, relying on her lights and siren to keep random citizens out of the way. As she came over the slight hill before Platt, she saw blue and red flashes, and she cut hard, sliding again, into the long service drive that allowed off-Packard parking for what was essentially an old-style strip development. She snapped quickly left to go parallel to the street and slid to a stop with her vehicle between her and the action.

The first officer on the scene was leaning over the hood of his car, pointing his pistol at a young white man, a man standing over the body of a woman. She was face down and screaming. The man was holding a dark revolver out from his side, at an angle to the ground, not pointing it at anyone. The officer was shouting at him to drop the gun, and the suspect was shouting incoherent defiance back at him. Jeri jumped out, went low on her hood too, and joined the chorus. In the background, sirens were on and getting closer.

Jeri's world began to slow down. She knew the feeling: tachypsychia. It can make time seem to pass slowly or with much greater speed, and she was experiencing the former. As she gradually adjusted her view over the sights of her sidearm, bringing the suspect's chest directly into the space covered by the rear notch and front blade, she felt almost calm. Her right index finger stretched forward alongside the trigger guard. And a voice in her right ear said "*Wait*."

That someone was speaking to her, in her head, didn't seem odd or surprising. In some distant place, she knew it was herself, the voice of training and discipline. But most of her consciousness accepted it as a benevolent spirit, guiding her through the hard bits of life. If she intellectualized it at all, it was to pay attention, to be confident in it. So she waited.

In the cold, snowy parking lot, no one else was getting any kind of guidance. The victim, so far unhurt but completely terrified, had no other idea than to shriek for help. The apparent perpetrator was so far gone in withdrawal that his only goal was to get away with the purse he'd grabbed, buy some heroin, and mellow out. The only clear thing, and the one thing that he was yelling at police, was a series of variations on the theme "I can't go to jail!"

The other officer, a man named Lagarde, stood up and took a step toward the suspect. He thought, he said later, that the subject was breaking, close to giving up. Instead, the suspect raised his gun and pointed it at Lagarde.

"*Now*," said the voice in Jeri's ear. She had time to smile, time to put her finger on the trigger of her Glock, time to shift the sight picture just slightly downward, and pull. Her target was standing with his left leg forward. Her round struck just above the pelvis, expanded, and tore through his intestines . He screamed, clapped his hand to his side, and dropped the revolver. Officer Lagarde froze. Jeri didn't. She ran around from behind the car and charged in. The suspect fell to his knees, but he turned right and started to fumble in the snow for his gun. Lagarde started to cover him, but Jeri was running in, closing on his line of fire. The man got ahold of the gun by its barrel, and started to turn back, trying to get a proper grip on it. Jeri's voice said "*Kick*."

She took one more step, planted her left foot, and swung the right forward in a *Mawashi Geri* kick. The heel of her boot took him directly on the side of his head and smashed a section of his skull. Her pivot foot slipped on the snow and she slid like a figure skater, in effect tripping over the man while moving backwards. The voice said "*Tuck*", but it was too late for that. She fell hard on her right arm, and she felt the wrist break.

The Emergency Room at the University hospital complex is large and imposing. Like most of its kind, its staff is heavy on nurses, interns, residents, and physician's assistants, light on full-fledged doctors. One of the latter was on duty on this gray Sunday morning, and she was dealing in strict sequence with three residents, each with a specific issue. She gave two of them their directions and turned to the third. "Yes?" she said.

"Well, there's a thing ... a question about that cop they brought in," he started. The surgeon was noted for focus. You got nothing from her until it was your turn, then it was all about you and your patient for as long as it took.

"The fracture? What about it?"

"Not the fracture. We've got that ... that's all dealt with. But she says she ..."

"She what?"

"She says she wants to talk to an oncologist. She says she has breast cancer."

"Explain." The surgeon could be a bit like MacArthur. They'd never met, but they had some of the same turns of phrase.

"She told me she'd been doing self-exams, and, um, she's got a lump that's getting bigger. And she hasn't seen anybody about it."

"*Semper aliquid novi,*" she thought. Always something new. "Okay, I guess we need to call the Cancer Center. Does she have a primary care physician?"

"She says no, Doctor. She says she hasn't seen anybody. She was, um, a little freaked out, until the sedation took hold."

"Why? Because she killed the other person they brought in?" The suspect's blood was on the gloves and gown the surgeon had just taken off.

"No, um, no, I don't think so. She didn't say anything about that. He died?"

"Yes, he did. Bled out from a GSW in the abdomen. Or a kick in the head. Either way, he was gone when he came in the door."

"Oh. So do I call or do ..."

"I'll do it. I know people over there. Give me her name and so on." She sighed. It had been a rough day already. Half of the city was slipping on the ice and breaking something. But a death certificate before noon on Sunday put her in a bad mood. "*It could be worse*," she thought. "*Much worse*."

Operating on the principle that it was always better to work from firsthand knowledge, she walked twenty feet down the row of patient beds; the occupied ones were closed off with curtains. She stopped at the last one, and knocked on the wall. Jeri Klein managed to say "Yes?"

"Hello," said the surgeon. "How are you feeling?"

"Alone," said Jeri.

The Sun Bear on the Record

The people in the room were mostly nervous. MacArthur was not. He'd given testimony, spoken under oath, signed affidavits and so on, probably more often than anyone else there, even Rusty Cornley's mother's attorney.

"All right," said that gentleman. "Now I think we can wrap this up with Mr. MacArthur, here. We've heard from the arresting officers, heard from at least one of the dispatchers. If we can just get Mr. MacArthur's input, we can call it a day." The large institutional clock said that it was nearly 4:00 PM.

The formalities took almost no time. The attorneys were used to depositions, the recording person was intensely familiar with them, and MacArthur was, too. He saw them as a great opportunity to shut up, to the extent that the questions would let you.

"Now, Mr. MacArthur, you are a ... let's see, retired member of the Ann Arbor Police Department?'

"Yes."

136

"But you were not involved in the arrest of my client?"

"That's correct."

"But you were there?"

"I was a witness, yes."

"How was that?"

"Coincidence. I happened to be present at the scene."

"I see. Uh, can you explain that a bit more?"

"I was getting coffee. Across the street. I heard the sirens coming."

"And you were interested, then?"

"Yes."

The clock said ten after four, and the attorney was getting tired of this whole thing. He knew already that Mac was just going to put one more nail in the coffin. His case was dead on arrival. He decided to cut it short.

"So you saw, personally, the events of my client's arrest?"

"Yes, I did."

"And ... ?"

"Can you be a bit more specific?" Mac asked. "*You get nothing for free, Sonny*", he thought.

"Would you just describe what you saw?" "*Come on, you old bastard. You know what I mean.*"

"Your client drove a car into the parking lot of the Starlight Plaza shopping center. It appeared to me to be out of control."

"And ...?"

"He exited the vehicle and began to walk towards me."

"Did he say anything to you?"

"He was speaking, but incoherently. I couldn't understand any of it. So I don't know if he was speaking to me." Mac paused, but the attorney was making a note, so he went on. He was as tired of this as anybody.

"He appeared to be distraught. He was bleeding from his head and from his left arm."

"Yes, all right. And then what happened?"

"As he walked toward me, an Ann Arbor patrol vehicle entered the lot. Officer Klein was driving it."

"What did she do?"

"She exited her vehicle, drew her sidearm, and pointed it at the subject ... at the plaintiff. She ordered him to stop."

"How did he respond?"

"He appeared not to hear. Not to notice her. He kept walking toward me."

"And then?"

"Another Ann Arbor vehicle entered the lot. That was officer Fraser."

"Mark Fraser?"

"Yes." Mac paused again, prompting the man to keep up the tempo. But he was fussing with his phone. Mac sighed and went on. "Officer Fraser exited his vehicle. He did not draw his sidearm, but instead ran to the plaintiff and placed him on the ground." Pause. "Officer Klein holstered her weapon and assisted in the arrest."

"All right, yes, that's consistent with their statements. Now, did you see my client holding a weapon?"

"No."

"Nothing that might look like a gun, for example?"

"I could see that he had nothing in his hands."

"Did you have reason to think he might be armed?"

"Oh, yes."

"Why?"

"I have an application on my phone that gives me ... that lets me hear emergency broadcasts. I was using that to hear what was being said about the pursuit of the plaintiff. From what I heard, I gathered the impression that the subject was armed."

"Okay, Mr. MacArthur, just a couple more questions, then. Do you believe that the officers ... Officer Klein and Officer Fraser, that is, also thought Mr. Cornley was armed?"

"I have no way of knowing that. But if I got that impression, then it was because I was hearing the same broadcasts they were. So I assume they did."

"Yes, right. So finally, then, as a retired law enforcement , uh, officer ... detective, do you believe that the arresting officers used reasonable force?"

Mac sighed again. His back hurt, and he was trying to keep his left hand from cramping up. He wanted to go the hell home, take a pill, and lie down. "Look," he said. "Both the officers in question carry nine millimeter automatic pistols. From personal knowledge, I know both their cars have shotguns. I have a concealed carry permit, and I had a handgun in my coat pocket. There were at least five semi-automatic weapons in that parking lot, leaving aside pepper spray and Asp batons. Only one weapon was drawn, and not a single shot was fired. Everyone involved, including an old retired beat up guy, heard those "may be armed" calls. The plaintiff had just hit and damn near killed a pedestrian. What I saw was a remarkably reasonable application of restraint. Frankly, he was lucky he didn't get shot." *"So much for knowing when to shut up,"* Mac thought.

"Yes, Mr. MacArthur. I see. I don't, um, I don't think I have anything more for you. Thank you."

The room emptied out. When he was alone, the attorney closed the door and called Rusty's mother. It took him five minutes to explain and then another five minutes to explain all over again, that he couldn't advise her to carry on with the suit. Besides having heard from everyone who might have anything to say about it that the police didn't abuse her boy, he also had a written statement from two internal medicine types saying that Rusty probably smashed his spleen on the steering column when he hit the curb. That and the shocking harm done to a young foreign woman would just about ...

"He never hit nobody," said Mrs. Cornley.

"But I'm afraid he did. I'm afraid we just can't get around that."

140

"He never did," she said again. She spoke in a low voice with no hysteria, no panic, just a grinding, implacable denial. "He never hit nobody."

"Well, if you can't accept the facts, I can't represent you."

"Yeah, that ain't a surprise. We're gettin' screwed again, I guess. But he never hit nobody."

Far inside the labyrinth, a long way from the halls and offices MacArthur knew, on a floor of patient rooms, the University's Acute Care Surgery group kept its trauma patients. Hee-sun Park lay there, still in an induced coma. They'd given her an IV port. Antibiotics, sedatives, pain medications, nutrition, a confusing and evolving set of fluids went into her body through a plug in her chest. Most of her head was covered with dressings. Her husband sat beside her, holding the hand that wasn't stabilized and pinned and restrained. He was asleep with his head resting on his free hand, and the tissue he still held was almost dry. Tears evaporate.

The Swift Fox and the Red Panda Bay at the Moon

Some people probably do fall in love very quickly. Others take years to figure it out. But if that represents some kind of normal distribution, then it follows that there's an average amount of time and at least three standard deviations from that norm. Andy and Jenn believed they were on the left side of the curve, and that by the time they were married, they'd achieved love. In fact, it took another week.

They'd had dinner at the Lime Inn. It was an old, long-standing place in Cruz Bay, one of a few restaurants with both local and tourist customers. It offered perfectly done fish and even a lobster or two when they were on hand; long-term employees;

and an evolved decor. The best part, though, was its horseshoe bar in the front and its bartenders. After ten o'clock, the barriers between staff and diners and bar customers blurred, and our couple had migrated from their table to the bar. They'd had wine with dinner, and now Jenn switched to Campari. Andy thought about it a moment and then ordered a Jameson. He could see a couple of bottles of it, standing on the back bar. It was well short of Saint Patrick's day, but the barkeeper took no chances with his inventory. You never knew when people might be celebrating early.

"Do you want that neat?"

"Straight up, yes, please."

On the other side of the horseshoe, two tourist couples were swaying back and forth with some piece of pop music that was on. It wound down, and the barman nodded at Andy's drink, made a quick esthetics-versus-tip calculation, and put on a Chieftains album. It was one of that old Irish band's guest recordings, and almost all the guests were sparkling women singers. The first track passed by most of the listeners; it was a little progressive for bar singing, and the barkeeper's intent was to get them singing. The next cut, though, was more successful than he could have predicted.

A Stór Mo Chroí means "you treasure of my heart", and Bonnie Raitt sang it with all the anguish of a woman seeing her love or her son going off to America. The slide guitar helped, but her voice was all that was really needed to turn this green island they were drinking on into another one, damp and chilly and far off to the northeast. There was a lot of staring down into drinks until Jenn straightened up and joined in. It wasn't perfect, but she had the advantage of knowing the words.

Andy had heard her sing before, but he felt as though he hadn't. Perhaps he'd never seen her before at all, quite so clearly. He knew at least a line of the last verse, and he joined in.

The bar man saw his mistake. He wanted them all singing and laughing, and if this went on, they'd all be in tears. He ran his eye over the CDs, and it fell on Christy Moore. There was a festival cut on it, essentially a Celtic rap, but the refrain was inescapable.

"Lisdoonvarna," said Andy to Jenn, but loud enough for the other side of the bar to hear. And as Mr. Moore went into his chorus, they sang along.

The second time around, the bar man and one of the tourists came in on it. By the end of the song, there were seven or eight voices. They were off and running now, and it took The House some fancy moves to keep the music going and the drinks coming. He found a Dubliners album and they sang the chorus to "Spanish Lady". The next one down the stack happened to be the Pogues, and he gave them "The Turkish Song of the Damned." Obscure, but again, the chorus was easy enough to pick up.

At the door, three young Japanese men looked in, a bit uncertain. "Come in, come in!" The bar was in a welcoming mood, and people moved around to make three stools available for them. "What are you drinking"? "It's on my tab!" "No, no, I'll get it!" The bar man had a brilliant thought, and he fished out the Chieftains again. "Here, listen to this!"

Toward the end of the album, some genius had thought of getting Akiko Yano to take part, and the cut is in Japanese. The young men's heads snapped up at the sound of "*Sake in the Jar*".

While it was playing, Andy ordered another drink, and he and the bar man had a brief word about the Christy Moore album. Andy pointed out a track and asked the man to put it on. Andy'd had two whiskeys now, and he was feeling either a new thing or remembering an old one. He couldn't have said which it was.

After the sake song, there was a minor distraction while the house tried to find actual sake. When it appeared, it was a somewhat low-end bottle, but the Japanese tourists still bought a round and drank theirs politely. They were somewhat behind the others, anyway. When Andy's song started, he stood up. Jenn looked at him, wondering what he'd asked for.

What he'd asked for was "*Vive the Quinte Brigada*", Moore's song about the Irish fighting and dying in Spain against Franco. Andy sang it along with Christy Moore. The talking and laughing stopped, and people listened. He had a better voice than anyone else in the bar, and he had another edge: he knew what the hell he was singing about.

The song names men from all over the Irish Republic, Frank Ryan, Charlie Donnelly, and more. It mentions fights that no one remembers, Villa del Rio for one, in a war overshadowed by the big war that followed. Andy knew the names, though, and he knew the battles. Jenn came in on the choruses, picking it up as she went. The others just listened; there was enough Spanish sprinkled around the lyrics to confuse those who were hearing it for the first time.

When it was over, the bartender was taken slightly off balance. There was a brief quiet spell. Andy sat back down, and the Japanese men asked for food menus. Andy looked at Jenn. And she stood up.

"Here's one," she said, maybe just a bit louder than was necessary.

"As I was comin' over, the far-famed Kerry mountains, I met with Captain Farrell, and money he was countin' ..."

"Whiskey in the jar," shouted one of the drunker tourists. "Not yet," said another one.

"Mush a ring, dumm do, dumm dah, wack fol the daddy-o, wack fol the daddy-o .."

"There's whiskey in the jar!" Everyone shouted the chorus. One of the Japanese fellows shouted "Sake!"

"And if he'll come with me, we'll go roamin' in Killkenny, and I'll engage he'll treat me better than me darlin', sportin' Jenny! Mush a ring, dumm do, dumm dah ..." Andy was on his feet, too, for the last verse and the mood was back. Jenn grabbed him, more or less gracefully, and gave him a long kiss. There was scattered applause.

"Friends!," she said." I give you the hottest Federal Agent in the Midwest, my colleague, and my partner, and incidentally, my husband! Agent Andrew McReady Patel!" She drained the last ounce of her drink.

"And gentlemen," said Andy, standing with some difficulty, supporting both himself and about fifty percent of Jenn. "Gentlemen, glasses please. I give you the loveliest Director of Corporate Security ... in the world! My darlin', sportin' Jenny!"

There were cheers and one or two of the waitresses looked in from the dining room to see what was up. Andy handed the bar man a substantial amount of money, and they walked out and into the tropical night.

The Least Weasel in Winter

Gerald's drive home was hellish. There was traffic and there was snow. He was late and ill, both in his head and in what he thought of as his soul. His mind flipped back and forth between two horrible notions. One: his employer, Gudrun "Mark" Bauer, was insane. Two: he wasn't. The evidence for the former hypothesis was compelling and based on personal observation. Gerald had sat with him and heard him outline a scheme to sell cut-rate respectability to the poor. To sell useless pieces of paper to anyone who, by definition, was foolish enough to buy them. And to hide the fraud behind a legalistic version of "*I never promised you a rose garden*".

On the other hand, Gerald's salary arrived in his bank account regularly. The lights in the FastFF building stayed on. He was in a position to know that the books balanced. People bought the company's existing offerings, and to date, no one had gone to jail over it. Bauer was making his demonic schemes work and making them profitable. And to Gerald, that was even worse than thinking of him as a psychopath.

He got a chilly reception from his wife. She objected to it when he was late, mostly because it complicated her somewhat offhand efforts at cooking. She heated up the lasagna for him, and they had a brief dinner together. They'd both been brought up to observe rigorous if middle-class table manners; neither one read or used a phone during the fifteen or twenty minutes that it took to eat. Gerald drank bottled water with his meals, and Alison usually had a glass of some inexpensive wine. Their conversations were limited to a few simple remarks about the weather or traffic or the local politics she dabbled in. Gerald's stock answer to anything about his work had atrophied long ago to a flat lie. "Nothing new." His head began to hurt acutely.

It was close to ten o'clock when they finished, and he retreated to his personal office. If he'd been a sports enthusiast or a hobbyist, it might have been a "den" or a "man cave." As it was, it looked more like the office of an attorney or an academic. It was lined on two sides with built-in bookshelves. There was a desk and a tablet computer, a window that looked out on the front yard, and low lighting. The lamps were all at head height or less; the ceiling light was never on.

Now, Gerald sat down at his desk with the lights dimmed down. His headache was becoming worse, and although he could see the hardbound titles on his shelves, he didn't try to read them. Most of them he knew anyway, just by the color of the binding. There were two bibles, a King James and a Douay–Rheims version. There was a copy of poor old Boethius' *The Consolation of Philosophy.* Not far away, there was Engels' *The Condition of the Working Class in England* and Mill's *On Liberty*. With conscious irony, Gerald had shelved it next to Paine's *Age of Reason*. The rows and rows of books went around the room, hiding their content behind cloth or stiff paper or even leather. Gerald started to get up, with the idea of consulting someone among the silent volumes, but the headache spiked, and he dropped back into the chair. He closed his eyes tightly and gripped his forehead.

The pain ebbed. He opened his eyes again, and he found himself looking out the window. The temperature had gone up a degree, and it was enough to turn sharp, hard flakes of snow into the larger, wetter fluff that falls slowly and accumulates. He thought about the master bathroom and the bottle of acetaminophen on the counter, but the idea of climbing the stairs was unpleasant. His wife came to the door and said goodnight in a formal way, and he waved his hand. It was nearly eleven now, and very dark outside. The snow was picking up.

He sat back in the chair and closed his eyes. Unwillingly, he thought of the decision he had to make. On one side, this house, this room, the books, heat and light and food. The luxury of thinking when there were things to be pondered. The horror of the work he did and the sheer effort of turning Bauer's plans into something that could be accomplished, regardless of the inherent evil. On the other hand, well, what was there? His dignity, maybe. Perhaps something like self-respect. He thought of the books; something like a soul?

With that thought, the pain shot up again. He curled forward, and his hands went up to his head. He was almost ready to call for Alison, but it stopped. He sat back again and actually lost consciousness for a few seconds. He was having a small stroke, his brain was receiving less blood flow than it needed, and it was beginning to shut down in certain parts. He sat there, his head cocked to one side, for three or four minutes more, and then his eyes opened again. He straightened up and saw the window. The snow was falling faster. He got up, supporting himself with the arms of the chair and then the edge of the desk. He swayed slightly, but he stood. Outside, a car went by.

Gerald turned, moving mechanically, doing one thing at a time. He walked out into the small entrance way of the house and opened the closet. He reached in without looking and took the first coat his hand touched. It was his raincoat. He put it on, opened the dead bolt on the door, and stepped outside.

The cold air was refreshing, and he looked with a blind, unreasoning pleasure at the snow. He moved forward, being careful without thinking about it, down the steps, down the walk, and onto the street. He turned, acting on instinct, to face away from the slight wind, and that pointed him southeast, following the darkness. Each time he thought of something, it was isolated and without premise or conclusion. Nothing came before or after; everything existed by itself, came from nowhere and lead nowhere.

He moved slowly, walking in the street. The snow came up over his shoes, but he never noticed. His eyes were locked straight ahead, and he was now counting, counting his steps, but only up to ten. Then he started over. He kept on.

After a few more minutes, he came to a large cross street. It was better lighted, but there was no more traffic now, at the beginning of a blizzard, than there had been in his neighborhood. He crossed without thinking about it, only looking for more darkness. Across the street, there was a small park. He walked through it, went down a slight incline, and kept going. He had no concern for it, but in fact he was now walking on the frozen surface of Lake Saint Clair.

Three miles straight ahead of him, a few lights flickered. The Canadian shore was populated and developed and people were at home, figuratively huddling against the storm. But the snow came and went between Gerald and the houses along Riverside Drive, and the lights looked as though they were signaling to him. He raised his head and looked up, and his foot went out from under him. He fell on his hips, and his head slammed down on the ice. Stars broke out in his vision. They danced along with the lights from Ontario, and Gerald danced along with them, lying still in the gathering snow. Slowly, the lights and the stars faded out, leaving just a cold darkness. Behind Gerald, his tracks were already covered, and now he began to be covered himself. The temperature fell, and the wind picked up. Gradually, Gerald became a snow drift.

The Sun Bear and the Northern Palm Squirrel in Symposium

"*He's not a complete loss*," thought MacArthur. He and Louie Burke were going to have another discussion, but this time Burke had gotten involved with something minor downtown, and he'd asked if Mac could meet him somewhere there. "Okay," Mac said, "Somewhere with coffee." To his surprise, Burke not only knew of cafes, he knew a decent one.

"So, Mr. MacArthur, it looks like things kind of ... moved on, on us."

"Come on, Burke. Call me Mac."

"Oh, okay. Sure. Anyway, we didn't really guess right about either of those cases."

"Really?"

"Not so much, no. The shooting one? You know, the drug dealer?"

"Yeah."

"His friend, the one who ran off and we couldn't find? We picked up a guy for a stolen car thing, and he said he'd tell us about the shooting. He said he was there and he ran, but he knew who the woman was."

"Let me guess. It was this Deano kid's mother, teaching him a lesson." Mac had at least one real guess, but he wasn't going to mention it. He assumed that if it had been Jeri Klein out there on the west side, waging her own war on drugs, he'd have heard about it by now, publically or otherwise. If it was any cop, for that matter, he'd have heard. Or an animal control officer. Or the mayor. So he breathed in and waited for Burke to tell him.

"No, it was his girlfriend. We're looking for her. She might have gone to Atlanta, the guy said."

Mac let out his breath. "Whose girlfriend?"

"Oh, Deano's. The guy who got shot. She was pissed at him for hanging out with somebody else."

"*Cherchez la femme*."

"What?"

"Never mind. And I suppose she had nothing to do with the butt pincher on Observatory?"

"No, not much chance, anyway. We went back and looked at the women he'd messed with. And we came up with one who lived right down the street. We interviewed her, and she was really, like, short with us. Just little "yes" or "no" answers. You know, "Have you seen your assailant since the incident where he touched you?" "No." "Not at all?" "No." Just like, closed up. But we checked a little more and guess what? She's a martial arts instructor! Chinese and Japanese styles. And even this Canadian thing, Lassavat."

"What? Canadian?" said Mac. "Say that again."

"Lassavat."

"*La Savate*. Yeah, not strictly Canadian, but French Canadian, sure."

"It's like kick fighting."

"Uh huh, and your witness said she kicked him."

"Right, but here's the other thing. He had these little scrapes on his forehead, kind of, uh, like maybe an animal clawed him?"

"Yeah."

"As we're walking out of her room, I look at her boots. She's got those ice gripper things strapped on 'em!"

"Ice cleats. Okay, good. Ice cleats, claw marks. I get it."

"And the witness girl ..."

"Woman."

"Okay, she said that the person *ran away* from the scene. But it was all iced up. So ..."

"So cleats. Yeah."

"We got nothing hard, but it just makes sense."

No, Mac thought, it didn't. How would she know he'd be hiding in the cemetery? That was the real problem. Of course, nothing except his general aversion to coincidences meant that she'd *have* to know. Or maybe *he* knew where *she* lived. Maybe he set the trap, not her. And it backfired on him.

"Well, except technically, it doesn't really matter," he said.

"You think so? I mean, he was a punk, for sure, but ..."

"Oh, it's not over, necessarily. You wait and see if your suspect does anything else. Any more ass kicking like that, and you know who to go back to. You file her away, and ... she's here for school?"

"Yeah."

"Maybe you file her a lot deeper when she gets done and leaves town. But you don't throw the information away."

Burke was still sipping on his tea-substance. Mac went up to the counter for another coffee. When he came back, he told Burke that the ice cleats were a good catch.

"Oh, thanks. The running away on the ice thing had been bugging me. But I got a question."

"Okay."

"It feels good, I guess, that the perv got beat up. And I kind of like ... I kind of want to not find out who beat him up."

"Me too."

"But is that, like, a bad thing?"

"Jesus, Burke. What am I, the Pope?" Burke's face fell, and Mac saw that there really was something under Burke's question. "*Oh, man,*" he thought. "*Burke. Irish, maybe? Was he brought up in the Church?*"

"Okay, let me try that one, but fair warning, this is gonna be long and snaky, as they say in Texas. You ever hear the old thing about how there are no atheists in foxholes?"

"What? No. Well, maybe. Like, from World War Two?"

"One of the world wars, anyway. What the people who cooked it up *meant* was that when you get into something really bad and out of your control, you turn to God. Everybody in combat, they were trying to say, is praying to somebody."

"Okay."

"But the thing is, it backfires on you. If you take it apart, what it really means is that when you lose all control, you start trying to influence things by believing in something." Burke looked blank.

"Here's what I mean. So the next shell to hit could be right on top of you, there in your foxhole, or it could hit the guy over there. And there's nothing you can do about it. So you suddenly become a Christian, or a Sikh, or a Buddhist, or a Jihadi. But you've been driven to it because you can't control the world. And the world could just swat you like a mosquito and never care. So you can panic and run, or you can stay in your hole and come up with a belief that makes you think you've got somebody looking out for you."

"Why's that a backfire?"

"Because it means that what you're believing is just ... comfort, I guess. And you come up with it or go back to it when you're in trouble. You use it when you're forced to. But it's not such an attractive product when life is okay."

"I don't know," said Burke. "I guess I get that part. But how does it ..." He made looking-for-the-word gestures.

"So how about there are no post-structuralists in court rooms?"

"Huh?"

"The guys who talk about how tables aren't really tables, just what we think tables are. And my table isn't necessarily the table you see. And it isn't the same table it was a second ago. Or in another universe. And if you hear me agree with you that it's a table, that could just be the me that you observe saying that."

154

"But, how ..."

"What I mean is, you can't use that kind of everything-is-everywhere idea on the job. Even if you decide you can't ever really prove something, ah, I guess you shouldn't take that thought to work with you if your job is proving things. You have to get up in the morning and think "*For the next eight hours, I'm going to pretend there's just one universe and just one reality.*" And at quitting time, you can go back to doubting things again."

"But are you saying that ... do you mean turn off what you think and turn it back on again?"

"Yeah, to some extent. You ever hear about fuzzy logic?"

"What?"

"It was a computer science thing. You don't hear a whole lot about it now, but you used to. It says truth doesn't have to be, ah, you know, digital. On or off. True or false. It says something can be zero true or one true or some number between. You can be half right. Or point-three-six-two right. And suppose you investigate something and give it a high value of truth. In court, that's called *beyond a reasonable doubt*."

"But if I charge somebody with something, I'm signing off that he did it. Not that he half did it."

"But at the bottom of it all, are you *sure*? In this and every other damn universe, you're *sure* he did it?"

"No. How would I know about the other ones, the other guys in other universes?"

"But you sign off, anyway. And the court agrees. And he goes to jail. In this universe. The way you see it."

"Yeah, because in this universe ... oh."

"Right. Because, *as far as you can tell*, he's in this universe and the court is and so are you. And he did it in this universe, so he pays for it here. You can *believe* anything you want here, and you can convince yourself that some of it is true enough that you're gonna say you *know* it, because you can see it and feel it *here*. And as you say, how would you know about the other ones? Sure, you can imagine the other universes, but there's no way in hell to know anything about them. Just this one, right? So I say, when somebody's out there in this universe, groping women's buttocks and getting his ass kicked for it, and we have laws that offer wiggle room to the people who did the ass kicking, I'm okay with letting them wiggle. As long as they don't make a habit of it."

"But ... still, the perv got hurt. He got hurt more than ..."

"Oh, man, don't go there. You're playin' right into their hands."

"Whose hands? What?" Burked looked around.

"The guys who think the reader is more important than the author. You say something and you mean something by it, but as soon as you say it, you lose control. And all that matters then is how I hear it. If I'm a cranky old retired guy, I hear it the way a cranky old retired guy would. Your victim hears it as "*I got beat up!*" I hear it as "*That'll teach him.*""

"That's weird."

"It's silly. All it says is "*People are different.*" My mother told me that."

Burke laughed. "Oh, man. I can see it. I'm going to walk into court one of these days and the defense is gonna say *Your honor, my client pleads innocent in another universe.*" And the Judge thinks that means something different than I do."

"And guess what? In some other universe, that already happened."

The Golden Jackal, The Black-footed Ferret, and The Rest Stop

Mark Bauer sat at his desk, staring at the back of his closed office door. Both arms were stretched out in front of him, resting on the surface. He was in the habit of sitting this way, easing the strain on his vertebrae. It forced him to keep the desktop clean, too. He was thinking hard.

Yesterday, right around three o'clock, things had taken a serious turn toward the dark side. Two young men from the Federal Bureau of Investigation had arrived, unannounced. They'd had a brief chat with him and with Pauleen Prenze, together, and they'd asked to see his Chief Financial Officer. That had been awkward.

"He isn't ... with us anymore."

"Mister Fisher Temple? I see his name on an office, though. He's still listed as ..."

"Yeah, I know. He just ... abandoned his position. He left and didn't call."

"That's called job abandonment," said Pauleen. "It's cause for termination."

"Well, okay," said Agent Patel. "But doesn't that concern you? Did you report that he was missing?"

Pauleen took over. She'd rehearsed this set of answers, quickly in the women's room, just a few minutes ago. "There were indications that he was unhappy with the job. We would normally have terminated him after forty-eight hours, but we gave him a week. To think it over."

"So you talked to him? You told him he had a week?"

"Ah, no. No, he didn't respond to calls. But we valued his contributions here, and we hoped, we really hoped that he'd change his mind."

"Okay, Ms. Prenze," said Peter Corcoran, "But ... I don't see why ... How long has he been gone?"

"Well, three weeks. Approximately. Exactly, in fact."

"So you didn't call anybody?"

"Oh, yes, of course. We called his wife. She didn't know where he was either. And she said she'd reported it to the Police, so ..." She left it hanging there.

"And you haven't noticed any irregularities? Or anything unusual, internally?" asked Andy.

"Well, yeah," said Bauer. "I mean, we looked at the books, and the accounts, and cash, and all that. Sure, we ..."

"We've conducted an investigation, internally," said Pauleen. "And I'm reviewing a proposal from our accountants to do their own." Actually, by tomorrow, she really would be, and it would be carefully backdated.

"But is there any ... are there any areas of concern?"

"Not to date, no. Nothing that would lead us to believe ..."

"We gotta be sure about that kind of stuff," said Bauer. "We have to know, for sure, before we can say anything."

"So, are you saying that you do think there may be a problem?"

"No. I'm sayin' we don't know yet." Corcoran was looking at Bauer, but Andy was watching Pauleen. He saw her give Bauer a quick, sharp look. But she didn't say anything.

It went on for a while longer. In their practiced fashion, neither of the agents revealed anything much at all about their visit or their investigation or if there *was* an investigation. They asked a couple of questions about the company's landlord, solely to leave behind a hope that they were looking at somebody else. It could have been any of Bauer's vendors; a red herring is a red herring. All they wanted was to leave the least possible amount of panic and evidence tampering in their wake. Instead, they left business cards and a polite request to hear about Mister Temple if he should be in contact.

They'd come in separate cars; there was no point in Andy driving back to Detroit and then back to Ann Arbor again. They stopped in the parking lot. "Bullshit," said Andy. "Yup," said Corcoran.

Upstairs, Bauer looked at Pauleen. "Bullshit," he said.

He'd thought about it all night, except for an hour or two of sleep. He carefully avoided doing anything at all out of the ordinary, anything that left a record or a trail. No pricing airline tickets for Argentina, no on-line searches for "hit man", no large movements of funds. Instead, he just thought, and by this morning he had an assessment of the situation and two or three specific things to get done. High on that list was having a secure conversation with Pauleen.

"*An hour's worth*," he thought. "*Maybe two*." In his mind, he drew an hour's driving radius around Ann Arbor. "*Lansing? Yeah, good. Maybe two and a half, going and coming*." He turned toward his laptop, and did a quick search for commercial real estate brokers in the capital area. He picked one at random, had a quick talk with an enthusiastic young man, and set up a visit to some mid-range office space. He got up and went to see his Admin.

"Pauleen in, yet?" he asked her.

"Her car just pulled in, Mister Bauer."

"Yeah. Two things, then. Tell her we're gonna go up to Lansing and look at that office I was talking to her about. And get me a rental car. Get 'em to bring it over here."

"A rental car ... yes, right away."

"Let me know when it's here."

In twenty-eight minutes, Pauleen Prenze walked out of the building with Bauer. They had exchanged fewer than a dozen words so far. He handed her the keys and said, "You drive, will ya?"

When they had the doors closed and the engine on, she said "What the fuck?" very clearly.

"Look," Bauer said, "We don't know dick yet. We don't know how long they been looking at us, we don't know what they know. From here on out, I don't trust my car, your car, my whole damn building. But somebody'd have to move real fast to wire a random rent-a-car."

"I see. Then what are we doing?"

160

"We're driving up to Lansing to see some real estate kid and some offices. We get some lunch and we come back. And we don't talk about anything but the goddamn weather except when we're in this car."

"All right. Do you care how we go? Twenty-three to Ninety-six?"

"Fine. I don't care. Just take your time. And don't go looking in the rear view mirror all the time. If there's somebody behind us, that's great. We'll waste a bunch of their gas, is all."

"So ... what are you thinking?"

"What am I thinking? I'll tell you what. I think there's only two ways to go on this."

"Only two? I could probably add to that," Pauleen said.

"I don't care. Listen to me on this, I been up all damn night chewing on it. One: Temple really did get killed or he got hurt or he ran off to someplace. That gives us a chance to grab some of the company's ordinary money and blame it on him. Right?"

"You would get caught at that so fast it'd make your head spin," she said, merging onto the highway.

"Maybe. But it's worse than that. Two: Temple didn't just go walkies, he's talking to the FBI. And they want us to do what I just said or something dumber."

"Yes. I thought about that. If we weren't taking this little drive, I'd be getting an audit in place right now, just for cover. And by the way, since we're talking ..."

"Yeah?"

"You really *don't* know where he is, right?"

161

"Nope. Do you?"

"No. So that's bad. So he might be talking to ... somebody."

"Right. But the good news is, unless you told him stuff, he only knows about the ordinary business and the ordinary money."

"Unless *you* told him, that's all he knows."

"Yeah, so if we clean up good, really good, the whole ordinary business looks all right, and the Feds quit listening to him."

"We can do that. The ordinary side is ... all right. We could get some bad press ..."

"We get that now. Who cares? But the other money and the other operations, how deep are they?"

"You know better than I do on that."

"Well, I think I oughta move it around some more. Make it harder to stumble on, you know? When you're looking for something else."

"Gerald didn't know about any of that." Pauleen felt cold. She did know, and she knew to at least the nearest hundred thousand dollars how much other money there was. But she didn't knew the details of how it was concealed. She didn't know how to get at it, how to draw from it, where the hell it was, frankly. Or what currency it was in.

"I think we need to be very sure we're in agreement about that," she said. "Very sure."

"Like what?"

"I need to sit with you somewhere and watch you do any moving around. I need to know, and I need to agree with it."

"Yeah. I see. You think I'm pulling out."

"Bauer," she said, "If you fuck with me, I'll cut off both your balls and feed them to the Agency."

"Likewise," said Bauer. They both stared straight ahead, Pauleen driving, Bauer just staring. "*Christ*," he thought, "*Why do I hire all these damn smart people?*" The last time he'd been worried by officialdom, it'd all been him. He could take the funds, close things down, and let the few remaining employees wonder why the door was locked on a Monday morning. This was a lot more complicated.

The car slowed and angled off to the right. "I have to use the rest room," Pauleen said. She brought the car onto the ramp for a rest area, coming down to twenty miles an hour and swinging around into a parking space. Bauer was taken slightly by surprise, and he didn't react instantly when she got out, taking her purse with her.

He sat there for almost five minutes before the fear broke out. She was away, probably in the ladies' room, probably calling somebody. And she had the keys. "*And I'm fucked!*" He jumped out and walked into the little building.

Rest stops on Michigan freeways follow a pattern, at least the newer ones. Cars are directed to one parking area, trucks and big motor homes go into another. Between them is a cross-shaped building with a central space and men's and women's facilities off to each side. Each end has an entrance. In one of the women's restrooms, Pauleen was trying to decide what in the hell to do.

The choices were limited. She could call one or the other of the Agents. She had no other contacts at the FBI. Calling some other law enforcement group was pointless; nobody was threatening her, she hadn't been assaulted or car jacked. Her lawyer? She didn't have one. She *was* a lawyer. And there was a limited amount of time left in which she could just walk back out of the bathroom and get back in the car with Bauer and go on with the whole thing. She didn't know that the time was already up.

There were just a few trucks on the truck parking side, and the car side was empty except for the rental. Bauer looked left and right, then walked into the building. He saw nobody, just two sets of bathrooms. He stopped and listened. There was no flushing and no sound of hand dryers. Nobody was talking to children, and nobody was walking on tile with heels. He drew in a breath, took a small automatic pistol out of his coat pocket, and walked into the nearest women's room.

Bauer had carried a gun for years. He'd bought it illegally, needless to say, and fired it exactly once, just to make sure he hadn't been screwed. For all the remaining years, the little flat .380 rode around in this coat pocket. This was the first time he'd ever thought about using it. He kept his right hand behind him as he moved forward. He had no clear idea what he'd actually do when he saw Pauleen, and so when he didn't see her, at the sinks or in any of the stalls, he was even more panicked. Then he realized that there had been two "Women" doors. She must be in the other one! He turned, his foot slipped, and he banged his hand on one of the steel dividers. It made a noise.

In the next bathroom, Pauleen had come to a conclusion. She had nothing she could do right now. In fact, she admitted, she'd really just wanted to get away for a minute and think. She'd go back out and pretend it was all okay. She walked through the door, turned to follow the dog-leg that kept people from seeing in, and collided with Bauer on his way in. A metallic object hit the floor and skittered away. "Shit!" she said. "*Gun!*" her brain said. She pushed Bauer away and ran, clumsily in her business heels, away toward the truck side entrance.

Bauer took two steps after her, doubled back to retrieve his pistol, and followed her out at a run. He went through the door and stopped. Ten feet ahead, Pauleen was standing, facing him. She had dropped her bag, and she had a small "*Ladysmith*" revolver in both hands. And most inconveniently, off to her right, there was a truck driver just getting out of his rig. Pauleen shouted at Bauer. "Forget it, Bauer! Forget it! I *will* fuck you up!"

Bauer raised his gun, too. The trucker's jaw dropped. He stepped down to the pavement and drew his own gun. Pauleen glanced quickly at him, then back at Bauer. The trucker yelled "What's goin' on!" Pauleen said, "He attacked me!" Bauer said "Get out of here! Get out!" Guns wavered around, shifting targets.

Meanwhile, on the car side of the lot, a mother pulled in. She got out and let her daughter run into the building. She herself stopped by the smoker's station, and started to dig for a cigarette. "*What's all that yelling?*" she thought. Her line of sight went diagonally past the building, past a couple of trees, over a table by the far sidewalk, and right through a triangle of angry, confused, and frightened people who were unintentionally reenacting a scene from *Reservoir Dogs*. Predictably, she screamed.

Without meaning to, Bauer jerked his trigger. The bullet went nowhere near Pauleen; it hit the right side mirror of the truck. The truck driver fired three rounds more or less at random, while dropping onto the snowy surface of the lot. He hit nothing, as far as anyone could later tell. Pauleen fired one shot at Bauer; unlike any of the others, she had actually practiced, and although the two-inch barrel threw high, she still managed to hit him in his forearm. She fired a second time, but the muzzle rise from the first shot sent this second round up and over the restroom roof, off into the firmament. The woman on the other side of the building screamed again and irrationally began to run *toward* the fracas, blindly looking for her child.

Bauer dropped his gun and clutched at his wound. The trucker was crawling around to the far side of his cab, fumbling for his phone. Pauleen took one look around, grabbed her purse, and realized that she had the keys to the rental. She ran around the building toward it and frightened the distraught mother even further. One of Pauleen's shoes came off in the snow, and she kicked off the other. She made it to the car, jerked the driver's door open, and got in. Fifteen minutes later, when the rest area was filling up with State and Sheriff's cars and an ambulance for Bauer, Pauleen was seventeen miles away, driving legally and carefully south down a two-lane highway.

The Mule in the Spring

The running and yelling and carrying was over. In the harbor, the ice was broken up and floating in a random jumble of blocks and pieces. It slopped against the moorings and against the side of the ship. The Waubuno's rudder was hard over to starboard, and her engine turned over slowly in reverse, swinging the bow out into the channel. She pivoted against the one remaining set of lines that held her stern to the dock, and as the bow reached the appropriate angle, the steering went amidships and the engine went to slow ahead. The last lines were cast off.

The Waubuno was an old girl, and except for electronics and communication gear, she was handled as ships were in the forties. She had a single rudder and a single propeller; her bridge was forward, looking out over the bow. Her long deck ran back hundreds of feet to a lower structure over the engines, and her stack rose from the middle of it. She looked like a ship, and she smoked like one, burning oil now instead of coal, but still leaving a black cloud as she moved out of the docks and into the lake. She followed another pair of vessels, a tug and a Coast Guard boat, as they bashed and bludgeoned ice out of the way. The winter was beginning to let go, but even in cleared channels, ice still formed overnight. The Waubuno was known for being one of the first ships to get out and working every spring, and this year, she was actually the first.

She went west on Lake Erie, moving slowly and stopping when the escorts stopped. They broke ice by moving back and forth, shifting sideways, pushing it away on either side. When it got dark enough that visibility vanished, they stopped again. Working their way ahead, they began the shipping season.

They came to the western end of the lake and turned north into the Detroit River. Two other ships joined them, working along in their path. The pace slowed down even more as they left the open lake. The channel between Grosse Isle and the Canadian side was narrow, and the effort to clear a path was demanding. Moving up river took time and concentration; and there were no ships to salute, docked at the industrial hell of Zug Island or in the mouths of the River Rouge. The convoy passed under the Ambassador Bridge, went by Belle Isle, and saw the banks of the river begin to open out and become Lake Saint Clair. It was getting dark again, and the Coast Guard ship in the lead was about to signal for a stop. The surface of the lake was a uniform white, covered with the shadows of snow drifts. The noise of breaking ice and broken ice banging against the hulls died away.

Gerald Temple's body, caked with snow, partly encased in ice, rolled over as it was broken away. It had little or no buoyancy, and it sank and floated, sank and floated until it stopped, partly jammed in the space between the Waubuno's propeller and her hull. There it stayed while the last light vanished, and there it was in the morning when the ships got underway again. It was held out of the way of the propeller blades, and as the boat went forward, it was pushed back against a support. When the ship stopped or went astern, the body was jammed against the hull. It waved in the currents of water, hanging in the dark beneath the boat. It was wedged in place, carried along day after day, as the ships passed through the lake, up into the Saint Clair River, under the Bluewater Bridge, and finally out into Lake Huron. Finally, a lurch of the ship against ice along the side of the cleared path shook it loose. It sank, bobbed up again, and was shoved down once more by the wake. It drifted down toward the bottom.

The lake bottom was rough limestone, covered with silt. A few miles away, it rose up and formed the Alpena-Amberley Ridge. Nine thousand years before, it had been a narrow land bridge across the lake, and there are still stone walls, now underwater, where Paleo-Indian people drove caribou into hunting traps. Gerald's body fell slowly down into a gap between rocks. It began the long process of becoming part of the lake, gaining a coating of sand and sediment, slowly falling away into its component parts.

Almost a hundred miles away, measured in a straight line northeast and through the channel into Georgian Bay, there was one of many small islands off the Canadian shore. In two cracks in the rock, you could see roots of old cedar trees, still holding the remains of stumps. Two hundred yards out, the bottom sand washed back and forth with the waves, and it sometimes uncovered a skeletal hand or a leg bone or the skull of a woman who had been on that rock, held in place between the trees until they died and splintered and fell and eventually floated off. In three hundred and thirty years, not much else had changed.

The Snow Leopard in the Spring

The Sault was full of people, and the shore was crowded with canoes. The sun was almost down, and the campfires were lit, all up and down the beach. An Odawa woman called Alsoomse was talking to a younger French/Mississasauga person she'd just met. This young wife was in her twenties and beginning to show a pregnancy, but to the older woman's private amusement, she still called herself an *oshkiniigikwe,* an adolescent girl. Her name, she said, was Marie, and she'd been raised in a white family, not far from Montreal. She spoke an Ojibwe dialect, but with an odd accent and more white ideas about age and place in life than a full-blooded Huron would have had. She'd just married, she said, back in the winter, and now she was here with her French husband, trading and talking.

Another woman walked by and said something. Alsoomse looked away. "Meskwaki," she said in an impolite tone.

"They come from a long way off, don't they?" Marie asked.

"They come to be unpleasant. But yes, from a long way off. To the west."

"Your people ... our people ... don't like them?"

"They aren't ... they always want ... I don't know, we don't get along. And your French people don't like them, either. The Meskwaki won't let the whites or us or anyone else go up their rivers, over there in the west. You watch, there'll be a fight."

"Now?"

"No, no. There are only four of them here. But in a few years, the *ogichidaag* will have to talk, and the French will have to talk, and then the canoes will go west."

169

"My husband has been off in the west. He says he's gone all the way along the shore of *Gichigamiing*. He says there's another lake farther than that. A long way off."

"That's not where the Meskwaki live. To go fight them, the canoes will go down this river, south and then west past *michilimackinac.* Then they'll find them on the other side of the great water."

"*Michigami?*", Marie asked.

"Yes. At the bottom of a long bay, the river starts, the one they think is all theirs. You watch, there'll be a fight about it."

The wind picked up, and it blew sand from the beach against them. They turned their backs to it and both looked up to see if the clouds were blowing away. There were stars beginning to show.

"You look at the lakes," Marie said, "And it looks like they go on forever."

"But they don't. They go on a long way, but they end. And the land starts again."

"Beaches like this, and then forests, my husband says. On and on."

"Sometimes, in some places, the forests stop. Then it's just grass and grass and grass. I was there once, with my people and some of yours. Just grasses. And *mashkode-bizhikiwag.*" Marie cocked her head. "The *bison,* you would say."

"Oh, the big cattle. Yes, my husband has seen them."

Alsoomse was getting a bit tired of hearing about the husband, but she was polite. "Where is he?" she asked.

"Right here," said Gaston behind them. He dropped his hands on Marie's shoulders. "You see, even in the dark, I know you." She took one of his hands and put it on her belly.

"In the dark, too well."

Alsoomse laughed. "*Not such a child, maybe*," she thought. "I was telling this young woman about where the Meskwaki live."

Marie turned around toward Gaston. "We were talking about the lakes and the land. Where do they end? Do you know where they end?" He looked up at the stars and then at the black water, showing just the slightest chop. One way down the beach there was an outbreak of angry barking as a dog warned another one away from his place by the fire. A smell of roasting venison and frying fish came with the wind from the other direction, covering the reek of drying beaver skin and unwashed people. There was singing in French and in at least two Algonquian dialects. A pair of tall pines leaned slightly against each other in the breeze. For some reason, he thought of the drowned woman on the rock.

"Why should it end?" he asked.

The Dall Sheep Goes South

Rusty Cornley shifted around in the seat, trying to get comfortable. He had a wadded-up shirt against the car window as a kind of pillow, but he was tired and stiff. His incision hurt. He was still groggy from his pain medications, and it helped make the passing Ohio scenery at least slightly more interesting. Miles of snowy corn fields flowed by, right out to the horizon. Once in a while, there'd be a crow or two, hopping around in the cornstalks, shoving the crusty snow aside, looking for corn kernels.

"Ma," he said.

"What?", said his mother. She was concentrating on her driving, staying in the right lane, keeping a solid sixty-five miles an hour. Another damn truck was coming up beside her, and she hated being passed as much as she did having to pass anybody herself.

"Ma, where are we going, again?"

"I told you three times already. Tennessee."

"Tennessee. Yeah, you told me."

Tennessee. Tennessee, where there was a sister of hers, where they'd stay for a while until they could get another place, another trailer or a duplex or something. Get a new account with the VA or the state or whatever. Get the boy his medicines. And get him away from those damn friends of his.

Medicines. She chewed on her lip. We gotta get him his medicines, and if we just go to a drugstore, they might be able to find out where he was. No, we gotta do something else. "*Hell*," she thought, "*If you can get illegal stuff on the street, you oughta be able to get regular medicine, too. We'll ask around.*"

Another truck came up , hung on her bumper until there was a decent passing interval, and then pulled out left. She ground her teeth. Damn trucks. Damn cops. Damn worthless, son-of-a-bitch lawyer. The hell with 'em all. Snow blew off the roof of a car ahead and splattered on her windshield. Damn snow. Damn winter. Back to Tennessee, back where it don't snow all the damn year around. Back where nobody'll try to say her poor half-bright boy ran over somebody. "*Michigan*," she thought. "*Fuck Michigan.*"

In the hospital room, Yee-Sun's husband jerked up in his chair. He looked at his wife closely, and then pushed the nurse button. A tall black woman responded within a few seconds.

"She said something" he told her. "I'm sure she spoke! Just now!"

The nurse ran her eyes over the monitors first. Then she bent over the patient. "Hello, Honey. You awake now?" One of Yee-Sun's eyes, the one not covered by her head dressings, fluttered slightly. Her lips moved, and she said something in Korean.

"What did she say," the nurse asked.

"Dreams," said the husband.

The Barefoot Weasel and the Sun Bear

"Mister MacArthur?" Mac was deeply involved with his phone, following a series of postings about feminism in science. He looked up and saw Jeri Klein standing by the chair. He was, yet again, waiting in the clinic for a blood draw.

"Klein," he said, "Hello. Didn't see you there."

"I thought it was you. Do you mind if I sit down?" She looked a little peaked, looked like a knife that needed sharpening. She was wearing civilian clothes, needless to say, and her hair was covered with the traditional chemotherapy scarf.

"Please do. So ... how are you?"

"Well," she started. "I guess ... I guess I'm all right." She didn't sound all right, not at all. "I wonder if I could ask you a few things."

"Sure," he said, not very sure at all, in fact. His involvement with her business had stopped abruptly with the Rusty Cornley suit. Her issues with the parking lot shooting were a closed book. "I don't know what I can tell you, actually ..."

"Can you just tell me how you reacted? How you felt about ... about it all?"

"Well, I guess ... I mean, I can't see any real problems for you. He had a gun. He pointed it at an officer, is what I hear. I don't see how you could have done anything else."

Her eyes opened wide. "What?"

"Isn't that what you meant?"

"The shooting? No, not that. Not at all. I mean how did you react to ... " She opened a plastic document folder and handed him a single sheet of paper. "To something like this?" It was a typical hospital outreach document, aimed at new cancer patients. The headline said "*So your body has betrayed you.*"

"Ah," said Mac. "I see."

"I don't see," Jeri said. "I don't know what to think about it."

"Okay, ah, let me think about it for a second." Mac was completely thrown. "*When the hell did I become anybody's spiritual advisor, acting, unpaid? First, it's existential investigation technique with Burke, and now it's dualism with Klein? Who am I, Oprah?*"

"So," he said, "I really don't think about being ... sick, I suppose you'd say ... that way at all. I don't think of my body betraying me. It's not a separate thing."

She cocked her head slightly, just like a puppy might. "You don't?"

"Well, no, I don't. I mean, you've got martial arts chops, right? Wasn't that part of whatever you studied?"

"Not in the Army, no. It was all about strength and skills and discipline, but ..."

"So you were in the Army? I didn't know that." Actually, he didn't know a damn thing about her.

"I got out. I couldn't stand ... I'm sorry, but I couldn't stand all the *men*. I was afraid I'd end up hurting somebody."

"*Right,*" Mac thought. "*Right. Absolutely. That makes so much sense.*" So much about her dropped into place with just that one idea.

"But," she went on, "Now I don't know what I'm going to do when ... when this is over." She made just the slightest gesture at her torso. "I don't know if I can go back into the Department or not."

Mac looked closely at her, more or less for the first time. Dark, dark brown eyes, very expressive. She'd be no good in an interrogation room, on either side of the table. She gave too much away, just by looking at you. And with that, an idea floated up. "You know, I wonder ... do you like dogs?"

"Dogs?"

"Yeah, dogs. You might do all right in a K9 role. Did you ever have dogs as a kid?"

"Yes we did. Big blue tick hounds, down in Virginia. My brother and I used to hunt with them."

"Well, think about that. I know some people in that end of things. I might be able to make some connections for you."

"Jerilynn?" said a technician. "Want to come on back now?" Jeri stood up, and Mac fumbled out one of his last leftover business cards. "Stay in touch with me," he said. "When you're back ... when you're ready to talk more, just let me know."

"Thank you. I will. And ... good luck."

"You too." He watched her walk away. *I am absolutely not licensed for this!*" he thought. But it was an attractive idea: Jeri Klein with a flashlight in one hand and a big, dark coated Shepherd on a leash in the other. *Hell, I'd drop the gun and get on the goddamn ground in a heartbeat.*

The Red Panda and the Lar Gibbon

Andy sat awkwardly on a couch. Between him and Alice there was a glass-topped coffee table, mostly covered with books and stapled documents. The spine of one large volume read *The Birth of Neolithic Britain.* A single printed page was draped over the book; it was an abstract from the *European Journal of Archaeology.* Alice was clearly nervous, and Andy wasn't especially comfortable, himself.

"Alice," he said, "I think Jenn Langton explained to you the ... the *connection* between your cousin and the Agency?"

"Yes, she did. And she said you'd want to talk to me."

"Right. And I'm sorry that we couldn't talk to you any sooner than this."

"I guess I understand that. In the sense that you had ... I think the term is an ongoing investigation?"

"That's correct. And now that the investigation has become public ..."

"I would say that people shooting at each other in a rest stop is fairly public." Alice kept her tone even, but a tang of sarcasm snuck in.

"It is, and let me say that it was totally unexpected. By us. We interviewed your cousin's company President and his Chief Operating Officer on the afternoon before, and we saw nothing exceptional. Well, except their ... except the *unconcern* they showed over Mr. Temple's absence."

"I see."

"But the unfortunate thing, unfortunate for us and for you, I mean, is that neither we nor they know where he is or what may have happened."

"You don't know?"

"No, no we don't. We were looking at him ... understand, not necessarily as any kind of suspect. But he was the CFO, after all. Of a company we had reason to suspect was doing questionable things. But we don't know where he is."

"And you think his company doesn't know either? Do you believe that?"

"It can be hard to separate the truth from what a suspect tells you, but I can say, just between us, privately, why we accept what they're telling us about your cousin."

"All right. I'd like to hear it."

"Fine." Andy paused, straightened his tie, and leaned back. "Before the incident, we really didn't have any clear evidence about that company. A number of reports, maybe. But they could have been disgruntled employees, customers ... you can't take that kind of thing as being conclusive."

"Okay."

"And so we went to see them, as an initial step. We tried to be non-threatening, and we didn't really ask them any hard questions. But we did ask about Mr. Temple, and we got answers that we felt were at least evasive."

"Evasive?"

"Well, he'd been absent from his job for three weeks. And all they'd done, they said, was call his wife. That seemed odd. We asked if they suspected any ... anything inappropriate on his part, and we didn't get any really concrete answer on that."

Alice straightened up. "Are you saying Gerald was stealing from the company?"

"No. I'm not saying that. Not at all. But he was the CFO, again, and if my CFO went missing, I'd certainly start an audit right away. But three weeks later, and they didn't know yet? That tells me they didn't find anything or what they found was something discreditable. To them. So, no, we don't have any serious reason to think that was the cause ... the reason he disappeared."

"All right. But this isn't making it clear why you believe ..."

"But now, they're not just vaguely suspected of shaky dealings. Now they're both under arrest. The President was hurt in the shooting, and the COO was arrested in Indiana a day afterward. They're both charged with any number of felony firearms violations. And they're both readily and willingly providing evidence against each other. Either one could blame Mr. Temple's ... absence ... on the other, but neither of them are. It would be in their interest to, and I can say that some of the things they're claiming about each other are ... damning, I

178

think, is the best way to put it. But they're not going into anything about your cousin."

Alice had been tensing up and even holding her breath. Now she breathed out and made an effort to relax. She didn't believe Gerald could do anything illegal. That would have been so completely and categorically against his nature, she thought. He would have hated even the idea of it ... and with that, another concept appeared. She needed a minute to sort it out, but it was there and coldly reasonable.

"All right," she said, "I got the impression you wanted to ask me some questions?" Andy had been watching her closely; the quick change didn't escape him.

"Yes, uh, I do have a few things I need to confirm with you."

"Go ahead, please. I'll do anything I can to help." The pat phrases gave her time to work through her new idea.

"All right, let's see. When was the last time you heard from Mr. Temple?"

"We had a phone conversation on Sunday. January fourth."

"Okay. That looks like ... like the day before his last day at the job. Did he tell you anything unusual? How did he sound?"

"He didn't sound ... I would say, any more unhappy than he ever did."

"What was he unhappy about?"

"Gerald was uncomfortable about doing the work he did. About being a finance manager. Executive, I guess, although he didn't use that word."

"Did he say anything that sounded like ... sounded like he was about to do something drastic? Did he say anything that you'd recognize later on as a goodbye or a justification?"

"No. He never said anything along those lines." She almost said "unless" or "except", but she kept her mouth closed.

Andy ran through a few more predictable questions, things about favorite vacation spots, people Gerald might have known, previous gaps in his life. Alice had, quite honestly, nothing much to offer him. He wrapped up. He'd gotten as much as he'd expected. There might be more in the future. This was a young woman, he guessed, who wouldn't let this drop. If she had some time to ponder, she might well have more to give.

"Agent Patel," she said, "Are we finished?"

"Yes, I think so. We may have some more questions for you later on. And of course, you can always contact me ..."

"Of course. But I have a question for you. Do *you* know where Gerald is?"

Andy stopped halfway up off the couch. He looked faintly ridiculous, bent from the waist with his arms hanging down. "I'm sorry," he said. "I thought you understood that. No, we don't. I don't."

"Well, then, think about this. What if Gerald left deliberately, but not because of what he might have done. What if that company made him literally sick?"

Andy sat back down. "I think we need to talk some more," he said.

When he got home, Jenn was there. They were already beginning to establish little greeting rituals, and when they'd gone through the hug and kiss at the door, Jenn stepped back and assessed him.

"You look like hell. I think you must have talked to Alice."

"I did," he said. "She's not especially happy."

"So what did she say? Come on, Agent Patel. The woman's my daughter in law, for some definition."

"Well, she thinks ... she thinks the company killed him. He was half-on, half-off with his personal philosophy, I guess. And he saw so much ghastly stuff, it made him sick."

"Sick? Like how, sick?"

"She thinks he had an attack of some kind. Physical or mental. She thought it didn't matter which. But it killed him, somehow, without anyone knowing."

"My, my," said Jenn. "That seems ... a little ... unusual. As a theory."

"I don't know. She's very good with words. She wrapped it up clearly, I thought."

"How?"

"She said he was fighting against his own nature. And he lost." There was a short silence. "Do you want to go somewhere for dinner?"

"Sure, Sweetie. Anywhere you want."

The Sun Bear's Walk in the Snow

MacArthur looked out his upstairs window with a harder expression than he'd normally wear. It was Wednesday afternoon, January 28th, and there was little snow actually falling. In a few minutes, it would be time to leave, and he took a last sip of his now-cold coffee. He set down the book he'd been reading, and went stumping down the stairs. The dogs were watching from the first floor as he descended.

At the closet, he pulled out his heavy and semi-respectable looking lined overcoat, put a pair of decent black gloves in a pocket, and once he'd shrugged the coat on over a sweater, added a dark fedora hat. He wound a scarf around the neck, kicked off his indoor shoes, and scuffed into his cleat-equipped boots. As he passed the coat rack, he picked out his good cane. The dogs followed him to the door, assuming a walk was in the cards. He slowly closed them inside, locked up, and turned to breathe in the weather.

It was cold, below freezing, and what snow was falling fell at a slant. He moved carefully, threading the dogleg steps down to the driveway, placing his cane at an angle where anything unfrozen presented itself. He used it for balance, primarily, and he was adept at finding the right places to brace himself.

He knew the route he wanted to take. North across his neighborhood, cutting through a grade school parking lot where cars couldn't, ending up on the crest of a hill below which he usually drove, ducking out onto Stadium and heading for the coffee drive through. This time, though, the intersection where he normally turned was actually the destination. He was doing something he seldom willingly did: second-guessing himself.

On the walk, he'd started to feel a slight headache, and making it up the little hill behind Saint Simplicius had winded him. So he paused, watching the cars turning into the lot, bottlenecking at the entrance, fanning back out to park. It was cold, and he started down the block slowly, wanting to go in at the last minute, with the last comers, hoping, actually, to have to stand.

He walked into the church just behind an older couple, waited until they turned right at the font and then went forward; he sat down in the last row. He remembered to uncover, and he propped his cane in a way that might discourage anyone else from joining him.

As his eyes adjusted, he remembered the room. He'd been there for a wedding or two, a few funerals. The architect was a local man, and he'd designed a catholic worship space with some lines from Asia and just a suggestion of modernism. Mac looked around at the other people. None of them seemed to be looking at the space.

The mass started with the usual tailing off of conversations and the opening words, but Mac couldn't hear any of it. He started to feel worse, and one set of eyes seemed to be taking in the bland, pale wooden arches and another mental camera to be playing back memories. His churches, as a boy, had been small, rough stone or brick places in the countryside. He'd been, as a man and an apostate, to cathedrals in France, Italy, London, Ireland. He had been in the Sainte Chapelle and roamed around the *Piazza dei Miracoli* in Pisa. What was being said, even the language being spoken here was incompatible with those images. And nothing at all was being said about the difference between those who are content and those who are miserable. An undeniable symptom appeared, and he swallowed hard.

He lasted eleven minutes. When the congregation rose for the first time, he picked up his stick and jammed his hat on. Ignoring anything else, Mac walked back out the doors and out of the church lot. It wasn't dark, there weren't enclosing woods, but it was a residential street , and he walked into the relative shelter of a large tree trunk. He leaned against it, struggled for a second, and vomited into the snow, gagging and making animal noises. *"Please, please,"* he thought, as he wrestled his breathing back into control. *"No children watching. No grannies walking pugs. I'm ten seconds, five seconds, ready to be a human again."*

He straightened up. He looked around in a guilty way, and tried to scrape snow onto the vomitus with the side of his boot. He was facing south, more or less by chance, and he just started walking home.

He passed back by the elementary school, descending the hill now. That had been a rare foolish thing to to do, he realized. Dangerous. And he saw also that it being the Old Church didn't matter at all. That could have been a Lutheran Synod or a Synagogue or a Madrasa or a Stupa. Or poor Alice Graves' Paleolithic Ness of Brodgar, for that matter. Anything at all that promoted a single truth to even a single questioning ear, he could again clearly see, was doomed always to do more harm than good, because of what happens when you say my truth is truer than yours, ye unbelievin' heathen bastard, you.

He stopped at the last street before home, wiping his eyes with a glove and generally getting a grip on himself. He straightened up, and felt a little better . *"Well,"* he thought, *"That wasn't it, anyway."*

Ten minutes later, he was sitting at the kitchen island, watching the dogs eat their lamb and sweet potato tartare. And out of his crowded, ill-organized dust bin of a brain, came a kind of salvation. Clear and colorful, it was the cover of a comic book. A desperate-looking person asks Robert Crumb's iconic guru character, "Mr. Natural! What does it all mean?" And the rotund, enigmatic holy man replies "Don't mean sheeit."

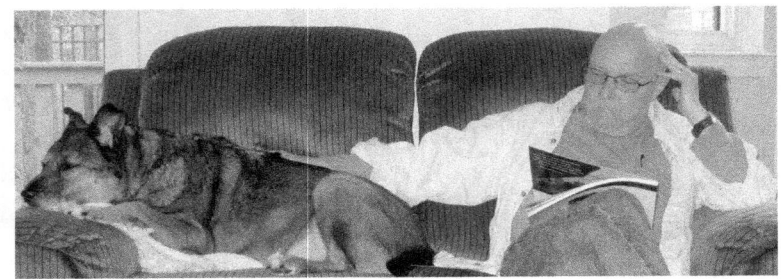

*Joseph McConnell describes himself as a retired technical bureaucrat. In and around his day jobs, he's been writing for decades, once sharing the cover of Whole Earth Review with Allen Ginsberg. Born in (extremely) rural Michigan, he's lived in Ann Arbor since 1977 and -- whether the city is prepared to admit it or not -- considers himself a stakeholder. **The Least Weasel** is his third novel.*

Other books by Joseph McConnell:

Many Believable Lies

Clash By Night

A Lair for the Wolves